I Have Three Things to Tell You, My Friend!

Revised and Edited - Second Edition

By
RM DAmato

I Have Three Things to Tell You, My Friend
Copyright © 2014 RM Damato

Oct-2014 Revised Edition

Cover design: Sara Galvis
Interior formatting: Veronica Yager

ISBN 978-1-62967-015-7
Library of Congress Control Number 2014934598

The best often die by their own hand
just to get away,
and those left behind
can never quite understand
why anybody
would ever want to
get away
from
them
– Charles Bukowski

Most men lead lives of quiet desperation and
go to the grave with the song still in them.
– Henry David Thoreau

Dedication

To my wife

and to

Teachers and school staff everywhere

Preface

I continue to call him Mr. Sinclair, even though by this time I am years older than he was when we first met.

I met him during the late summer season, when life is rich and the voices of decay begin their siren call. He became my mentor when I first accepted the teaching internship from the university soon after the Federal Rehabilitation Amendment had been passed. The rest of the story will unfold later, but we met at my first crossroad in life. In fact, he helped to create that dynamic event in my life. The second crossroad took me away from teaching and made me an artist and historian, living off a miserly federal stipend with no prospect of a second career. Others like me usually wait for an early and natural death.

Maybe, in some unknown fashion, Mr. Sinclair helped me to be honest. I cannot change the circumstances of his last minutes, but I can recount my version. So, after a lifetime of notes, journals, conversations, confiscated material, and gossip, I have compiled a record of his last school year and my first school year. The lies will persist, but so does cancer. Some will accuse me of lying, but the past cannot be completely and factually true in the present. It is an honest representation from my perspective. The historian must find the best semblance of truth. I owe it to his memory. He was my friend.

He may have been my only, true friend.

Prologue

August 1983

John Sinclair sat anxiously on a plastic chair, wedged among a line of teacher recruits in the bowels of a dilapidated post-depression building.

The Los Angeles School District headquarters housed a long entourage of teacher recruits who passed the California Basic Skills Test in 1983. It was the last week of August and school would begin in one week. None of them had ever taught or had any teaching training. The candidates—some in their twenties, others far into middle age and looking for a second or third career—had volunteered for an experiment.

California, especially Los Angeles, desperately needed teachers to fill swelling classrooms of immigrant and migrant students. When the universities had failed to recruit and train an adequate supply of teachers, the state resorted to enticing civilians via an easy credentialing process and a secure paycheck, along with a pension and medical benefits. In the middle of a deep recession during the waning days of the Cold War, what more could any confused, drifting college graduate need? Besides, anyone could teach.

Really . . .?

More than 50 percent failed a basic skills test and, out of the remaining 50 percent, 80 percent would drop out of teaching in the next five years. Why? The economy improved until the crash of '87.

Whoops!

Neither the state, nor the district succeeded in maintaining a steady contingency of teachers, as the revolving-door recruits would swing through the district's portal of complacency and contempt. Every recruit knew the secret truth no one mentioned or shared.

2

Teachers were a disrespected lot. But in public forums, the hypocritical platitudes swelled to offensive heights. No one cared if teachers succeeded, and most people expected them to fail. In 1983, they were the intellectual fodder for the social canons of apathy—just a plug filling the growing gap of educational mediocrity.

But to John Sinclair, it was an appropriate stopgap, a stepping stone job. Nineteen thousand dollars and three months off would carry him into his next position. The career he really wanted. For most of the emergency-credentialed teachers, labeled the second career recruits, teaching offered them that bridge. Some wanted to be actors; some wanted to be writers; some wanted to be policemen. All wanted to be someone—anyone better than a teacher.

Teaching didn't pay. Teaching lacked fame and glory.

John looked to the left of his seat and saw a long line of recruits stretching out to the exit where they waited to be interviewed. Most of them were men, but sprinkled here and there were a few women. Unlike the men, most of the women had earned their credentials while completing their bachelor's degrees.

John was lucky. A district clerk had mistakenly taken the middle cadre and moved it forward, to the chagrin of the others. After a few quiet buzzes of complaints, everyone fell silent again and returned to the private anxiety of waiting in front of testy, bureaucratic officials. Sinclair then looked to his right and saw three clerks beginning to interview several scores of untested individuals.

"We got lucky," the person on his right spoke up. "I'm Bill."

"John," Sinclair responded, dipping his head and smiling uneasily. Somewhere in the background, a ghetto blaster played Blondie's "Heart of Glass."

Bill was an older man, probably in his thirties. He wore a white, threadbare shirt and a thin, polyester tie. The knot of the tie, carelessly made, hung an inch below the collar button. He had brown eyes, yellow teeth, a receding hairline and a pockmarked face. Occasionally, he would look down at his blue, paper folder that he clutched on his lap. Although seemingly expecting to elicit a response from Sinclair, none was forthcoming. He then disappointingly opened his folder, extracting his transcripts, several identification papers, and his test results.

"You'd think they wanted us for the CIA," Bill complained. "After all this," and he waved his folder at the gathered room filled with people, "they want us fingerprinted. Damn."

"It's the kids," Sinclair pointed out. "They don't want perverts or deviants."

"Check it out," Bill remarked and pointed his folder at the others. "Who are they shitin' with?"

The other recruits heard the defamatory statement but decided to ignore it. Like Sinclair, they felt the same dislike for Bill. But they had learned it was best to ignore most unpleasant comments and events. Maybe they will just go away, . . . maybe everything was all just a bad dream.

Sinclair also ignored him and unconsciously glanced at his pack, which sat at his feet. He could not find a folder or professional briefcase for the interview. All he had was the simple backpack he had used in graduate school.

"I am applying for a job at CBS," Bill quietly confided to Sinclair. His breath reeked of tobacco and decade-old plaque. "This is just a gig. You know."

"Yeah," Sinclair answered and moved slightly to his left.

"What you teaching?" Bill demanded to know, shoving the papers back in his folder. "I got chemistry in West Los Angeles. Not a bad place."

"English," Sinclair admitted, taking an aching look in the direction of a nearby clerk's desk, where the employee was concluding her interview with a middle-aged woman.

"English?" he skeptically repeated.

"ESL," Sinclair blurted. "I got picked up in the valley."

"Hah!" Bill burst out. "You got fucked royal. All the wetback and slope boat kids are going to be bused there. You'll have your hands full. '*My name is . . . I live in a house . . . I want to be an American*' Ha!"

The clerk stopped her interview to stare at Bill, who was laughing to himself as he returned to his folder and the pointless task of shuffling his papers.

He remained silent for the next ten minutes, but then suddenly, the long, grumpy line of recruits made an uneasy movement to the left and then to the right before breaking in two and allowing a TV reporter and cameraman to enter the small lobby.

"Oh, shit," he cursed, as they entered the crowded vestibule. "I hate these people."

"I thought you wanted to work at CBS," Sinclair retorted mischievously.

"Yeah, man," Bill responded spontaneously. "Only on the other side of the camera. Anyway, they're shit independents. Channel 9." With that, he held up the folder to his face as the cameraman began to pan across the room.

The cameraman made several sweeps from one recruit to another and finally landed on Sinclair, where he focused the camera directly in front of his face. Bill abruptly stood up and walked away. Next to the cameraman, a middle-aged male reporter with a shoe-polish comb-over shoved his microphone into Sinclair's face.

"Why do you want to be a teacher?" the reporter demanded to know.

The glaring camera light annoyed Sinclair, and he looked away towards the other recruits who stood to his right. Then with a smile he responded, "I think I can help," as he made an effort to focus on the reporter and away from the camera's light.

"And what about the future of teaching?" the reporter quickly followed up.

Sinclair looked at the recruits and paused for a few seconds. "Well," he began judiciously. "In my opinion, the demand will decline."

"Can you explain what you mean?" the reporter pressed on. Then he nervously looked for another recruit to interview, while still holding the microphone to Sinclair's face.

"Yeah," Sinclair offered a prediction. "We will become an endangered species in the next century. Machines will take over. Ideas won't matter. Performance alone will count."

The reporter skeptically gaped at Sinclair and immediately pulled his microphone away. The cameraman religiously followed the direction of the microphone, and the camera's light bounced off the wall several times before landing on a pasty young face.

"Do you think your pay is fair?" the reporter asked the young recruits at the other end of the hallway.

Sinclair could not hear the response.

Brusquely, his neighbor returned and barely retrieved his seat from another approaching recruit who attempted to sit down next to Sinclair. Bill glared at him, and he angrily lumbered away.

"I heard you," he spoke in an accusatory tone. "Shit! . . . Look around here. They'll need us forever."

"No, the system will find a way to whittle us down. It's the nature of the machine."

"Nah, they will always need us. See! ESL dupes like you. *'This is a pen. This is a piece of chalk,'*" he said, continuing to wave his folder mockingly as if it were a baton.

He continued until an authoritative voice interrupted him.

"John Sinclair?' the female clerk called out.

Surprised, Sinclair looked up and watched a conservatively dressed woman wave him over to her desk.

"Good luck," Bill halfheartedly said, needing to get in a final annoying comment. Sinclair walked over to the clerk and heard his neighbor's mocking voice pursuing his steps. "*I have a book,*" Bill repeated with a false Spanish accent. "*My name is José. My papa, he do the garden work.*"

A shrill laugh beat him to the clerk's desk.

Chapter 1

August 2023
Smith

"I have three things to tell you, my friend!"
—Fernando Smith (The Janitor)

He sat alone in the dark and counted his keys. The bastard, Rubio, once again withheld the supply closet's biometric key.

"Son of a bitch!" Smith cursed his supervisor. "Motherfucker!"

He furiously shook his cracked dustpan at the indifferent gods.

Chapter 2

August 2023
Sinclair

Time passed and Sinclair discovered how much he enjoyed teaching. Much too quickly he was approaching his final year. He would miss the classroom.

When he entered the National Retirement Rehabilitation building, Sinclair expected to witness an advanced twenty-first century institute that matched the revolutionary biomechanical technology that initiated and maintained its existence. His arrival caused him to experience an anticlimactic catharsis.

"This is fucking progress?" he quipped out loud.

The building had been a food depository warehouse on the outskirts of downtown Los Angeles near some railway yards of transportation grids. Brown, sooty bricks covered the face of the edifice, and a modern sign barely disguised a century-old whitewash company label. Sinclair looked at the building after he had parked his car at a charge station and paid for his electrical allowance, He felt as if he had been sold to the glue factory. Besides the sign and the state-of-the-art charging station, only a sophisticated tinted film masked the building's interior occupants and activities from nearby or distant prying eyes. Sinclair appreciated the irony that in the shadow of the ten-story behemoth stood a modern, medical facility, which used green energy power for heating and cooling.

"Wow!" Sinclair said aloud to himself as he looked at the pristine medical building. "I hope this isn't something out of *The Jungle*. What crap!"

Staring at the building, he thought about the life-changing events taking place inside. His wife, Rachel, would be taking the same enhancements as he would to begin a new career in the medical field. Unlike his wife, he didn't know the profession he would choose since he felt so much at home with being a teacher. But he had always had an affinity for building machines. Secretly, Sinclair knew his relationship with Rachel teetered on their ability to reenergize the once red-hot spark that had fizzled from their union. Economic circumstances and the corruption of a much-too-comfortable life had prevented them from seeking a divorce. Their children had grown up and were no longer a factor in any of their decisions. So, after decades of marriage, they had basically become bored with one another. Rachel encouraged Sinclair to accept the enhancement with a faint promise that they might be able to mend their relationship. Sinclair still loved her, but he was uncertain if he would wish to live another half century, or even a full century, with an unfaithful woman.

Also, he thought about his next—and final—school district assignment: mentoring a student-teacher at Ulysses High School. Sinclair would be given a light teaching load as he prepared for his next career. Later in the day he would meet with the new teacher, a Mr. Sanchez, he thought. He vaguely remembered the name. He was never good with names.

Sinclair then walked up to the building's blackened glass door, which automatically opened. A young woman dressed as a nurse greeted him at the doorway. She looked perfect—her body displayed every nanotechnical and genetic enhancement that science could provide. The nurse looked like a forty-year-old at the age of 120. Too bad for her! A few feet behind her, Sinclair noticed two testosterone-augmented security guards with high-voltage stunners on their belts.

"Mr. Sinclair?" the young woman cordially greeted him. She was following protocol with her cynical, polite greeting. Since he arrived at the facility, the face-recognition software identified Sinclair 100 feet before he reached the entrance.

"Yeah," Sinclair grunted and walked past the grinning mannequin of a woman.

"We have been waiting," she continued to speak. "You are most fortunate. Dr. Ishido will join your team today. How wonderful."

"Thrilling," Sinclair answered in a barely audible voice. "Isn't it?"

The nurse deeply disturbed him, and he secretly believed that she was not human. Maybe a DNA freak or automaton would lead him to his doom. Inside, a narrow, abandoned lobby, no more than seven feet wide, ran perpendicular to the entrance. The sterile, light blue walls created an atmosphere of claustrophobia, despite the hidden presence of a large bureaucracy. Sinclair followed the nurse, and at the same time he sensed that the guards were keeping a close watch. Turning, he noticed that one guard had shifted his position to observe him as he and the nurse walked towards their appointment room.

"Hey," Sinclair called out in a nervous attempt to calm his nerves, "where's the rest of the facility?"

The nurse ignored the question, and she suddenly stopped and pointed to an unmarked door. "Thank you, Mr. Sinclair," she said. "We are here."

"We are?" he asked, regarding the door's peculiarity. A hair-thin line between the door and the wall frame gave a faint hint of the presence of a door. No knob, hinge, or label revealed its existence.

"Have a prosperous day," the nurse wished him as the door slid effortlessly to the right. "Your social contributions will be rewarded."

Without waiting for him to respond, she walked away—her measured steps, like the ticking of a metronome, carrying her down the hallway in the direction of the guards. Only the guards' distant backsides were visible as they turned to eye the nurse. They had lost interest in Sinclair.

"Wow," he surmised. "If I were them, I'd stare at her, too." Nevertheless, he was not fooled into believing that no one was observing him.

"Come in," a paternalistic voice welcomed Sinclair into the seemingly vacant room.

Sinclair could not see anyone as with dread he walked into a yellow room that was furnished with a large, black granite table, sitting below a wide-screen monitor. Two young doctors and one young female attorney sat, leaning back in soft, blue leather chairs behind the august table. One man was Caucasian, and the other was Asian. The woman appeared to be of mixed race, showing more Asian traits. Except for their gender differences, they appeared indistinct, and Sinclair would have difficulty identifying them in a classic, police lineup. With current technology, the effort would be unnecessary and counterproductive.

"Sit, please," the Asian doctor kindly offered a seat to Sinclair.

Another blue leather lounge chair appeared from an opening in the floor and swiveled in Sinclair's direction.

"Let me introduce myself," the Asian doctor began. "I am Dr. . . ."

"Ishido," Sinclair interrupted him as he sat in the chair.

Once Sinclair sat down, the chair slowly swerved again to face the three-person committee.

Dr. Ishido amicably smiled at Sinclair and looked down at the granite table, where Sinclair noticed there was a flat-screen tabletop monitor. "Your wife, Rachel, was here a few days ago," he commented, as he looked at the tabletop screen. "She is a teacher, too. Charming woman; it was a pleasure to meet her."

"If you say so," Sinclair replied, dismissing the compliment since he knew how most men reacted towards Rachel.

"And," Ishido continued, without losing his stride. "You have two children. One boy is an accountant, and the girl is a graphic artist."

"Lucky me," Sinclair said, hoping to avoid saying anything more about his children.

Ishido maintained a pleasant grin on his face and looked down at the screen again. "Identify," he commanded.

"John Sinclair," the computer spoke in a gender-neutral voice. "Born in the class of 1958. Caucasian. Optimal health for his genetic state. No enhancement present. Only medical stabilizers. Advancing signs of genetic degradation. Physical and mental acumen at ninety percent. Profession: teacher . . ."

"Enough," Sinclair shouted, startling the rehabilitation stewards. "We all know this, . . . don't we?"

Ishido stared at him for a moment and then gave him an indulging wide smile.

"Shall I continue?" the computer demanded to know.

"No," Ishido dismissed the request with the same controlling, paternalistic voice. "Mr. Sinclair knows his status very well, as do we."

He nodded to Sinclair who only blinked back. Shocked, the other administrators showed a sudden crease in their medically-enhanced faces.

"We understand," Ishido tried to comfort Sinclair. "We have been in your place. It's good when all this passes through its process. We were in our nineties and now function like we're in our twenties. It's a marvelous journey of regeneration."

"Yes," Sinclair answered, wondering if Ishido's ability to hold an erection had improved, too. He wanted to ask but bit his tongue instead. "I hear this all the time."

"Fine," Ishido concluded. "Let me introduce my colleagues."

At once, Sinclair noticed the glaring synthetic beauty of the woman, and, although rationally he accepted her age as ninety-plus, his subconscious dismissed it as a forgery of nature. She could not be that old. He knew the news stories were true, but he still could not accept the complete reality of the science. His generation significantly benefitted from the medical and social revolution of Rehabilitation.

"This is Dr. Schopenhauer," Ishido introduced the man next to him.

The doctor stiffly smiled.

"And to your right is the Center's legal counsel," he continued, uninterrupted. "Ms. Joan Fischer. She will explain the obvious legal issues."

"I see," Sinclair muttered apprehensively. Inwardly he felt like screaming and stampeding out the door towards the guards, where he would grab their stunners and commit hara-kiri.

"First," Ishido spoke softly, "do you have any questions?"

"Only," Sinclair spoke tersely, "tell me the facts. That's all I want. Take out the art and drama."

"Well . . ." Ishido appeared to be miffed since he often prefaced his litany with a history of the science of rehabilitation.

Schopenhauer noticed the tension between the two men, and he intervened. "Let me proceed," he suggested. Ishido silently bequeathed his position. "You are very lucky to have Dr. Ishido here. With your outstanding record, his presence is an honor.

"I'm sure," Sinclair responded. "You see, . . . I just want to know what I need to know. That's all."

"OK," Schopenhauer acquiesced. With a silent nod, Ishido and Fischer gave him their express approval to proceed.

"Let's begin," he announced. As Sinclair's impatience mounted, Schopenhauer explained, "First, our counselor will present the legal stipulations."

Fischer smiled and began to tap the table. A screen activated in front of Sinclair. "Today, Mr. Sinclair," she explained in a factual tone, "you will sign a preliminary agreement of understanding. The final agreement will be completed at the end of your school year."

Looking at the documents on his screen, he already knew their contents, after having spoken to his attorney and the district's union representatives. All this formality annoyed him, but the process was a legal necessity.

"As you can see," she spelled out the agreement, "you will begin the enhancement process so your body is in optimal health. The medical procedure will not reverse the aging process. Only slow it down. You will agree to the stabilizing of your condition."

"Yes," Dr. Ishido added, deciding to speak again. He assumed his paternalistic expression again. "We must make sure all of your vitals are optimal. You may eat normally but must not take any medicine or drug without the Institute's approval. No alcohol or cigarettes. If you do, the process is void."

The attorney pointed to the signature line on the table. Sinclair slowly picked up a stylus and digitally signed the document.

"I am aware of all this," Sinclair wearily informed them. "But what will I feel this year?"

Dr. Ishido looked at his colleagues and raised his hand. "You," he proclaimed with a biblical tone, "will be in perfect health! You will still be sixty-five but feel like forty. It will last you until eighty as you continue to age. But this will be easy as you have no major illnesses and your DNA tests show no aberrations."

"Of course," Schopenhauer gravely reminded Sinclair, "if you don't proceed with enhancement, you can't pass eighty." Sinclair knew the benefits came with a price.

"You will live a very healthy and comfortable life," Ishido added.

"But voluntary retirement is eighty," Fischer emphasized.

Sinclair understood the euphemism for death. Euthanasia! All retirees who did not volunteer for enhancement and a second career faced legal, government death. The economic system could not support the medical expenditures of a lifespan beyond eighty when the health stabilizers began to collapse and the human body succumbed to entropy and expensive treatments.

"So," Sinclair asked the obvious, "when do I begin?"

"Now," Ishido confirmed gleefully. "I suppose you don't wish to see the video?"

"No," Sinclair declined and lied, "I saw it at school."

"Right," Ishido condescendingly added. "You're a teacher."

"One more item," Fischer gently interrupted Ishido. "You must choose a second career. After the enhancements, you will have to enter the university and be reeducated for a new career. I hope you didn't plan to continue to teach?"

"No," Sinclair answered, knowing that he was obligated to choose a different career. "I've been told teaching would no longer be an option."

"So," Schopenhauer probed, "what is your second career? You indicated mechanical engineering. We have no more information yet. It must be interesting? With your background, you can choose to do anything you wish. Even become a doctor."

"Not really," Sinclair rejected the subtle offer. "That's for my stuck-up wife."

Schopenhauer appeared to be taken back by the rejection.

Ishido again took command of the situation. "You have time to decide," Ishido insincerely comforted Sinclair. "A psychologist will assist you and meet with you throughout the year."

At that moment, a slender robot with various appendages appeared through another seamless door and rolled up to Sinclair's chair. One of the appendages moved towards Sinclair and halted next to his right arm.

"You will receive a battery of shots and may feel ill for a couple of days. Nothing that will incapacitate you," Ishido explained. "But by the end of the week, you will begin to feel younger. This will be your most productive year as a teacher. You will work at an optimal state." He stopped to read his screen. "Congratulations! You are slated to receive the state's teacher career award and will be given mentoring assignments for the next generation of teachers."

"Yes. It's all about production and working at an optimal state," Sinclair sardonically commented.

Ishido's friendly composure evaporated, and he looked down at his screen. "I'll make your appointment with the psychologist next week," he decided without looking up at Sinclair. "And your career counselor. Have you done anything related to engineering lately?"

"I plan to," Sinclair offered without any details. "A package is coming by way of UPS."

Ishido leaned back and thoughtfully studied him. Sinclair did not hazard an explanation. "Smart man," he thought to himself.

"Any questions?" Schopenhauer asked as the robot maneuvered Sinclair's arm into a position for his battery of injections.

"I have an appointment later," Sinclair reminded them of his meeting with a student teacher. "At the school this afternoon."

"You will be unconscious for a couple hours," Ishido assured him. "And will recover in time for the meeting. If not, . . . you can meet later. They should understand, and you have your legal rights."

"Anything else?" Schopenhauer asked once more, expressing his impatience with Sinclair.

"How does it feel to be young again?" Sinclair demanded to know. "Really young! Not just healthy and dandy."

They all looked at one another, and Ishido's smile returned.

"Marvelous," Ishido proclaimed.

The robot then began to deliver its shots.

"Does it still feel real?" Sinclair pressed his questions. "I'd like to know what it feels to be in a rebuilt body with an old mind and soul."

"The soul is not a factor in the enhancement," Sinclair heard Ishido's last response as his consciousness faded under the effects of the medicine coursing through his veins.

"I always knew I had no soul," Sinclair managed to mumble as his vision tunneled out. "Damn. I should have had a drink." He passed out without hearing an answer to his question.

Chapter 3

August 2023
Sanchez

Brandon Sanchez sat in front of Dr. Pierce, the director of Ulysses High School. He was a thin, formally dressed young man in his early twenties, with long black hair and deep dark eyes. Pierce, formerly known as a principal—apparently a passé title for a director—had Sanchez's file open on his tablet. He was dressed in a custom-tailored white suit, yellow shirt and black tie. His long, angular face and bushy eyebrows moved in synchronicity with his eye movements, as he scanned the new employee's information. The meeting was taking place in the conference room since Pierce's office was being upgraded and fitted with an improved Smart Board. Compared to the capabilities of the Smart Board, Pierce felt as if he were currently using a wax tablet from ancient Rome.

The conference room was a bare green room, and in the far corner hung an early Smart Board prototype. Sanchez, having taken a quick tour of the campus, noticed a strange contrast between the obsolete and the state-of-the art. Each piece of technology that had been requisitioned reflected a teacher's particular status—whether he or she was in good standing with Pierce and the district. Noticing its meager décor, Sanchez assumed that the staff, and in particular Pierce, held the conference room in low esteem. An extended, gray Formica table stretched across the conference room and almost came to rest against a series of long, tinted glass windows. Sunlight peeked through the narrow windows, striking the Smart Board and revealing its ancient yellow cracked frame.

Finally looking up, as if suddenly remembering that Sanchez was in the room, Pierce asked curtly, "Did you like the tour of our school?"

"Interesting," Sanchez feigned. "So much has changed since I was in high school not too long ago."

Pierce remained silent as he studied his tablet and once again ignored that Sanchez was present. Then, as if to acknowledge the intrusion, he remarked, "Well, I'm sure it has. I had planned to show you a Prezi presentation on my board." Pierce, his brows lined up like little soldiers, looked up at Sanchez and motioned to the ramshackle Smart Board in the corner. "We're having technical difficulty," he continued in a tense tone, "as you can see . . ."

"It's fine," Sanchez assured him and looked apprehensively at Pierce's tablet.

Pierce followed Sanchez's glance and instinctively moved in closer. "You have an interesting history," Pierce spoke without looking as his recruit.

Sanchez remained quiet.

"Well," Pierce added, "you graduated summa cum laude in social studies with a minor in philosophy. I see you received a master's degree also. Congratulations." He then looked up at Sanchez who tried to show some excitement. "Looks like you did voluntary domestic service at the urban youth camps for two years." He stared into Sanchez's eyes. "Brave man," he half-joked. "I am glad you survived."

"It had its rewards," Sanchez admitted, offering a measly smile, "and its challenges."

Pierce studied him for a second and returned to the tablet. "I'm sure," he commented without looking up. "Then you applied for law school and received a ninety percentile score. Admirable."

"But I was put on the waiting list," Sanchez reluctantly clarified.

"Unfortunate," Pierce spoke unconvincingly. "I see that here. Interesting, even with your high recommendations." He looked up and smiled stoically at Sanchez. "Their loss is our gain," he admitted and returned to his tablet.

Sanchez began to feel uneasy in his chair.

"So you will be with us for a year," Pierce concluded. "Probationary."

"Yes, Pierce," Sanchez wanted to move the conversation along. "The law school said I must wait for the next cycle of applicants."

"Of course," Pierce responded condescendingly and swiped a quick glance at his tablet before slightly raising his voice. "But I think we can convince you to be a teacher."

He studied Sanchez's face, which showed the strain of an approaching yawn.

"Yes," he convinced himself, feeling the welling of a yawn, too. "You will be assigned to a social science virtual school lab. American and European history. You will guide and coach tenth- and eleventh-graders."

"I understand," Sanchez replied, accepting the assignment reluctantly as he tried not to show his reservations. Sanchez wanted a real teaching job. Most lecturing positions had vanished on the secondary level. A learning lab, which dominated the curriculum of most secondary schools, provided little to no stimulation for the teacher.

"No, you don't," Pierce corrected him and offered a friendly smile. "I have a surprise." He waited for some interest to appear in Sanchez's impassive face.

Sanchez was concerned.

"Well," he regrouped his pitch. "You will be able to lecture, too. A political science course for dual enrollment students."

The word, 'lecture,' caused Sanchez to sit up. His unexpected reaction seemed to please Pierce.

"And," he added like a pitchman at a carnival event, "your students will be given college credit. It will be an officially accredited course. Your mentor will be Mr. Sinclair. He is our most esteemed and experienced teacher. Maybe he can convince you to take up this profession."

Sanchez felt relieved and could not believe he was being given a lecturing position, even if it was one class. Law school could certainly wait.

"So," Pierce proclaimed, "doesn't that sound ducky?"

"Quack," Sanchez blurted out and chortled.

They both laughed.

Pierce studied him, as he tried to decide whether Sanchez approved or disapproved. Was Sanchez mocking him or cheering him? He sometimes had a difficult time interpreting people's reactions, and his therapist had told him to count to twenty before responding.

"Yes," Sanchez said, realizing his discomfort. "It sounds great. Really!"

"Ah," Pierce felt suddenly relieved. "Well, . . . let's go on." He again studied his tablet. His face expressed sudden disappointment.

"I have a message that Mr. Sinclair cannot join us today," he said. "Some issue with his rehabilitation therapy. Too bad. He is making the retirement transition this year, you know."

"I understand," Sanchez tried to sound sympathetic. Deep down, he felt uneasy. Sinclair's absence could possibly affect his chance to teach.

"I'll arrange for you to meet him in person later in the week," Pierce assured Sanchez. "He is very affable. But sometimes he is a little short-tempered." He watched Sanchez's reaction and then laughed. "It goes with his age, I suppose," he continued with a giggle, and his eyebrows twitched with glee. "Sinclair is a really strong individual—nothing to worry about. These treatments are a little rough in the beginning."

"I'm sure," Sanchez answered, beginning to wonder what sort of menagerie he was entering. Despite his fear and apprehensions, the offer of a lecture class erased any reservations he had about teaching for the school year.

"So," Pierce added, "how does your family or significant other feel about this? I know it's not the most popular profession these days. Many see it as a dead end. I still have faith in it."

Pierce thoughtfully looked over at the old Smart Board and then turned his attention to Sanchez. "It was such a good presentation," he half-apologized. "You would have seen what I meant. Maybe for next time?"

"Oh," Sanchez thought about his husband, Nick. "He will like the idea. I was brought up to like teachers and education."

Unlike Sanchez, Nick had made it into law school, and he disapproved of Sanchez's selection of a teaching career. They had met their first year at college and always had been on the same path. This year things changed. Nick had other wishes for Sanchez. They often spoke of a business partnership after law school. As for Sanchez, he now was unsure about a legal career with his lover.

"I'm sure my family and partner will like my teaching a lecture class," Sanchez lied. "I can't wait to talk theory to the students." In truth, Sanchez had always had romantic notions of speaking to a willing audience about political theories.

"Good," Pierce approved and continued to study his tablet. Sanchez waited for him to add more information. A long silence passed.

"Well," he finally spoke, "we need to sign off on the paperwork and get your computer access codes." He raised his eyes to Sanchez. "You wonder why we still call it paperwork?" he mused humorously. "Nothing is done with paper anymore . . . you know, environmentally hazardous." He snickered, and Sanchez joined him with a wide smile.

"So," Pierce changed his tone, "do you have any questions?"

"No," he answered, desperate to get out. "All is good for me." With that Sanchez's phone began to vibrate. Pierce frowned.

"So," he rose to indicate the close of the meeting. "Please see my secretary before you leave, and the paperwork . . . that word again," he guffawed. "Paperwork. Make sure everything is signed."

With that, Pierce offered his hand, and Sanchez shook it. "Good luck," Pierce told him and walked out of the room as he laughed to himself.

Sanchez was not sure if he were still laughing at the word "paperwork" or at the offer of "luck." When Pierce was safely out of view, Sanchez called his partner.

"You got the job?" Nick asked.

"Yeah," he answered, keeping his voice down. "It's a real lecture job—rare as chicken lips to get this for my first year on the job. Cool?"

Nick ignored his excitement and jumped in with another proposal. "I got a possible job here for you as a legal clerk," he said, hoping to persuade Sanchez away from the teaching position. "It's only for a year and then . . . law school awaits you. You'll only be one year behind me."

"Yeah," Sanchez prepared himself to turn it down. "You're not listening. I got a lecture job." There was a loud silence on the other end of the phone. "I don't want to be a clerk."

"You know, you are a faggot," Nick shouted angrily.

"So are you," Sanchez indignantly retorted.

"Fuck off!" Nick shouted. "You don't give a shit about our business."

Before Sanchez could respond, Nick hung up. Sanchez stared angrily for a moment at the phone. A middle-aged woman walked by and stopped to look into the conference room. "Everything OK?" she asked.

"Oh, yes," Sanchez smiled and happily waved his phone. She smiled back and walked away. "Welcome to the great vocation of teaching," he sadly concluded. He walked off to complete the paperwork, which awaited him in the next room.

August Intermission

After recovering for two days, Sinclair decided to skip the first week of preparations and faculty meetings. Ishido's shots caused an unexpected reaction, but when the flu-like symptoms dissipated, Sinclair felt as if he were twenty-five years younger. His memory worked with more clarity, and he had more stamina.

Pierce had spoken to his wife and sent him a virtual get-well wish. He also received a message from the new teacher, Sanchez, and he promised himself to call the neophyte before school began. He continued to doubt whether he should proceed with the rehabilitation process, but the UPS box in the garage immediately allayed his more serious doubts.

Using a box cutter, Sinclair sliced open the box. Inside the corrugated box from Canada, he found natural fiber Styrofoam and recycled paper obscuring the contents. He quickly removed the packaging and threw it aside. Then, he carefully pulled out the plastic bag containing an 80cc two-stroke refurbished engine to be attached to a mountain bike. They had been banned for twenty years, but a technicality allowed the engine to be mounted on a conventional bike, if it were refurbished in its original condition.

Compared to the original cost of the engine, Sinclair had paid at least ten times its value. The rest of the box contained the gas tank, spark plug, chain, gears, wires, harnesses, throttles, and all the necessary accessories. Sinclair used the box cutter again to free the components. Admiring the parts, he held up the 6-horsepower engine. Then, he stood up and walked to the refurbished mountain bike, as he measured the height of the engine inside the bike's frame. It fit!

"You two want a room together?" a sardonic female voice asked. Rachel's shrill voice startled him and broke his reverie.

Looking up, he noticed her standing by the garage door. She was wearing a green business suit and carrying a large simulated leather handbag. For her age, she looked a decade younger; the rehabilitation treatments had had a dramatic effect on her appearance and acumen. "No," Sinclair turned his eyes away. Her presence diminished his enjoyment of the project. "Just checking out the initial fit."

"It's legal?" she questioned seriously.

"Yes," Sinclair answered annoyed. "I went over the law and have the original certification. It will be fine."

"I don't want the police to call," Rachel jibed. Sinclair ignored her. "Where are you going to get the fuel?"

"It's been modified to run on pure ethanol," Sinclair murmured.

Sinclair could hear her sigh with defeated resignation.

A moment of silence regenerated her resolve. "Well," she warned him, "I don't want to smell it in here."

Sinclair ignored her again for a moment, as he took the engine out of the frame and moved it back to the box. He reminded himself that he would need to purchase flat-free tires for the bike, if he were to run it over 30 mph.

"I'm leaving," Rachel declared perfunctorily. "Going to the mall to shop for my trip next week. Yes."

"OK," Sinclair said, not wishing to enter into a discussion and wanting to return to his motorbike.

"Do you need anything for next week when I'm gone?" she proceeded. "You do remember I'm doing an exchange program in Japan for several months?"

"I'll be fine," Sinclair said. He kept wishing her away as he carefully packaged the engine in the box. Sinclair could feel her need to leave him behind as soon as possible, which was very agreeable to him.

"Fine," she repeated, taking a long look at Sinclair. "You know, this bike will be good for you, now that I think of it." Her comment surprised him, and he turned his attention towards her. "You see the bike . . . and your new career in engineering. This will complement your decision."

"Yeah," Sinclair agreed, returning his attention back to the box. He liked the bike and engine but was not convinced about a new career in engineering. "Maybe," he thought quietly.

"Don't forget to call that new teacher," Rachel reminded him. "His name is . . ."

"Sanchez," he interrupted her. "Thanks."

She then looked at him and the box and decided not to make any more comments. "Bye," she added and disappeared.

When Sinclair heard her drive off, he opened the box and pulled the engine out. Then a memory from his past struck him. Rachel's green dress reminded him of another young teacher, Sophie, who visited on an exchange program from Brazil. She was wearing a green dress when she first met Sinclair at a department meeting. The bright green color of the dress accentuated her round hips and braless bust and added an exotic glow to her light coffee complexion. The memory strongly affected him so long after he thought he had forgotten the details. Its sudden reappearance and emotional impact startled him. "I really forgot how beautiful she was. She was beautiful from the moment she introduced herself to her American colleagues," he mused.

Although they never spoke at the first meeting, Sinclair immediately fell in love. He replayed the scene in his mind. "It's the damn shots," Sinclair concluded irritably. "What a bitch it is to grow younger!"

———————

Nick left him alone to work on his lesson plan for the first day. Although he had not met Sinclair, the online textbooks gave him a clear agenda concerning the material that needed to be taught. Sanchez hated to be unprepared for any task. As he reviewed the curriculum, a summer school classmate sent him a text message with an attachment. He opened it and saw his summer school classmates—all newly recruited teachers, posing with their education professors. Sadly, he only remembered three names out of forty students, including the person who sent him the message.

"Why did they take the picture?" he asked himself.

The moment the photo was taken, Sanchez had wanted to escape from group. The futility of the photo annoyed him since he would almost never communicate with any of the student teachers or instructors again. The photographer had coerced everyone into posing for the photo. Sanchez closely studied his portrait and tried to read his face, as if he were looking at a stranger. He only saw impatience and artificial congeniality in his small features. Then, he looked to see who sent the photo. Like the people in the photo, the e-mail contained only aliases. Without regret, Sanchez simply deleted everything and returned his attention to the curriculum. Maybe the photo would resurface when he reached his rehabilitation in forty years.

"Further useless endeavor," he concluded to himself.

His mind then focused on his first probable lecture, while feelings of excitement and apprehension swept through him.

———————

Fernando Smith waited for a response from the Rehabilitation Committee. His paperwork sat in limbo, and he desperately wanted to begin his retraining for a second career. His job as a janitor had been unfulfilling and humiliating, especially since he lost his last job at a resort. Deep down, Smith wanted to return to the resort, and he secretly planned a path towards his goal. After a one-hour wait, a female clerk, dressed in a bright yellow smock, paged him to come to one of the little nameless windows in the cavernous reception room of the Rehabilitation Center. He hoped he would have time enough to return to work. Smith did not want to have a confrontation after having received another write-up from his supervisor, Rubio.

Startled upright—he had almost dozed off—Smith walked nervously to window 18.2. "Yes," he said, trying to make a good impression by offering the clerk his most friendly smile.

The clerk glared at him through her round-framed dark-tinted glasses, and then she glanced down at her monitor screen, which was out of Smith's view. "Your paperwork is incomplete," she blurted.

"What?" Smith questioned automatically. Her pronouncement seemed unreal. He had made every effort to submit his application accurately and rapidly.

"You can't meet with the committee until the paperwork is complete," she impassively explained.

"What?" Smith could only repeat. He felt nauseous. "What's wrong?"

"You see," the clerk impatiently pointed out, "we don't have all the responses."

"Responses?" Smith asked, feeling the bile rise to his throat. "What do you mean?"

"Your supervisor," the clerk explained, raising her voice an octave. "Mr. Rubio has not submitted his document."

"¡No me digas! Don't tell me!" Smith looked around him and felt anger quickly overwhelm his fear and timidity.

The clerk watched him nervously.

"Rubio?" Smith spoke accusingly.

"Yes," the clerk spoke in exasperation. "Tell him to submit the answers."

Smith did not respond to her last comment, as he stormed out of the reception room. When he stepped outside, and faced the dreary parking lot under the colorless Los Angeles sky, he began to scream and stomp his feet. "You bastard," he cursed. "You're fucking with me on purpose. I'll kill you. Puto! You faggot!"

Smith stormed off, leaving others who entered and exited the Rehabilitation Center flabbergasted and perplexed at his loud, vengeful rancor.

"Puto!" he kept repeating loudly as he walked to the door. "First, he has to sign the paperwork."

The fact that he had to return to work with a broken dustpan added more irritation to his plight. Luckily, everyone stayed out of the way of the cantankerous little man.

"That puto!" Smith kept shouting, holding up an imaginary broken dustpan, as he walked towards his late-model car. "No," dismissing his vow. "First! Rubio will give me a new dustpan. Justice is justice."

Chapter 4

September 2023
Sinclair

"One. I wish you a lonely death."
—Fernando Smith (The Janitor)

It was Thursday in the late afternoon. Sinclair was sitting in an office, as he waited for his rehabilitation counselor who was was late for the session. While waiting, Sinclair tried to put the first week of school out of his mind, except for the meeting with the new teacher, Sanchez, the next day. He had had little contact with the young man, just an exchange of a few pleasantries. Assigning Sanchez the mundane work of supervising the Social Science Laboratory, Sinclair had made him a promise to allow him the opportunity to lecture after he set up his small cadre of students. Sanchez seemed disappointed, and Sinclair suspected that Sanchez had believed he would be able to lecture during the first week.

He promised himself to address these issues tomorrow. Overall, he liked the new teacher, despite wishing to dissuade him from pursuing education. Outside school, he had contended with a few small glitches in his motorbike and the ill-fitting clamping devices for the engine. All of these thoughts whirled around his head, including thoughts about his wife's impending departure for Japan.

When the counselor entered the room, Sinclair suddenly became aware of the office décor. He was sitting behind a large, mahogany desk that shielded a red leather chair. On the desk sat a computer tablet and a phone. The rest of the room contained bookshelves filled with old books and antique objects, including a nonfunctioning

AT&T dial phone and a GE desk fan. A cool, blue color tinted the walls of the tightly compact room. A narrow window, looking out on a garden, split the room in half and allowed ambient light to escape through the gaps in the white, vertical blinds.

"Sorry I'm late," the counselor apologized, extending his hand to Sinclair. "I am Mr. Vega."

Sinclair smiled and shook his hand. Vega quickly sat at his desk and turned on his tablet, waiting for it to boot up so he could sign in.

"Good," he said with satisfaction, after successfully signing in. "How are you?"

"Fine," Sinclair answered.

Vega was a short man who seemed to be physically swallowed by the tall red leather chair. He had a thin goatee and was practically bald. His kind, reassuring hazel eyes peered out through a pair of round, black spectacles.

"Your room is interesting," Sinclair mentioned, pointing to the different antique objects. "I actually used these things as a kid."

Sinclair then pointed at a vacuum tube RCA radio with an alarm clock.

"I love collecting antiques," Vega admitted proudly. "You should see my house. My wife always tells me some of it has to go." He then laughed at his domestic story, and Sinclair made an effort to smile at the personal joke.

"Yes," Sinclair understood, thinking about his motorbike and his own wife's objection to the hobby.

"Mr. Sinclair," Vega began in an encouraging tone. "I am here to help you make your choice." Sinclair's smile melted, but Vega kept his own friendly demeanor. "We need to meet every other week," he continued. "Is Thursday fine?"

"Sure," Sinclair agreed uneasily. He did not like to talk about the rehabilitation process and career choices, but he had no option now.

"I am not here to judge you," the counselor clarified. "Everything is confidential, and the Rehabilitation Committee does not receive a report—unless there are serious concerns. You understand? Concerns, such as ongoing issues that would affect your long-term mental health."

Sinclair remained silent and watched the previous glee in Vega's eyes diminish a bit.

"So," he pressed on. "I have no preset questions or agenda. We are here to talk about anything that comes to mind. Right?"

"OK," Sinclair attempted to be conciliatory.

"Good." Vega's kindhearted demeanor returned. "Do you have any thoughts you want to share first?"

He waited as Sinclair tried to prioritize his thoughts and select the one he wished to reveal.

"How do you feel after receiving your first rehabilitation shots?" Vega asked, taking the initiative. "A little sick?"

Sinclair watched Vega who showed serious interest. "A little," Sinclair admitted. "It's kind of like the flu. But I am better now."

Vega nodded sympathetically. "Yes," he showed his compassion by extending his open hand. "You will have some ups and downs. The school is supportive?"

"Yes," Sinclair told him. "They told me to list my absences this school year as rehabilitation illness."

"Right," Vega spoke authoritatively. "It is your legal right. You know it all, I assume?"

"Of course," Sinclair spoke, wanting to retreat.

Vega rubbed his goatee as he observed Sinclair. "OK. Let's begin with a simple question today. . . ..How do you feel about choosing a new career and accepting these changes?"

Sinclair began to sweat and remained silent as he reviewed the feelings he had suppressed for so long; this wasn't going to be easy. Vega just patiently waited and leaned back in his chair. "I feel," Sinclair tried to force the words out of his mouth, ". . . confused."

Vega continued to wait silently, providing facial encouragement for Sinclair to continue with his thoughts. "I don't know if I want to go through with this," Sinclair blurted out.

The counselor gave Sinclair a compassionate expression and leaned a little closer. "You mean the second career option?" Vega clarified.

Sinclair nodded in the affirmative.

"Is it a lack of interest?" Vega searched.

"No," he disagreed. "I like engineering, I think."

"Engineering," Vega repeated. He briefly looked at his tablet. "You are a social scientist. Interesting."

"I am putting a motorbike together," Sinclair added as an explanation. "It's not the hobby. It is the life choice I have to make."

"How so?" Vega searched for more substantive reasons.

"I am tired," Sinclair divulged. "Tired of life. I don't know if I want to continue for another seventy years of life and a second career." The effort to make the admission left him feeling a bone-deep exhaustion. A trickle of sweat dripped down his backside.

"Life is tiring," Vega agreed. "I think what you're probably feeling is the consequence of your age. I've heard this before. When the rehabilitation regimen takes effect, the fatigue and aches will evaporate. You'll have the physical and mental energy you had forty years ago. I can almost guarantee you'll have a different perspective in the near future."

"But," Sinclair interrupted and stopped speaking. His thoughts and feelings were in conflict, and he felt as if he were in a cloud of confusion.

"Yes?" Vega waited patiently.

"What if it's more than that?" Sinclair pushed. "What if I am just sick of life?"

Vega studied him for a long moment before he spoke slowly and clearly. "Could be," he tried to be conciliatory. "How's your relationship with your wife?"

"Not good," Sinclair admitted. "She's leaving for Japan. It's part of her transition to the medical field."

"I see," Vega answered understandingly. "So you'll be alone for some time."

"Yes."

Vega made some notes in his tablet. "Children?" Vega asked, making further notes on his tablet.

"Grown up and out of town," he announced. "They have their own lives and relationships. You know how it is."

"Of course," Vega spoke congenially. "Any close friends?"

"Not many. I am a loner for the most part."

"I see," Vega thought for a moment. "Well. We can't explore all of this now. I would like to address these feelings you have, talk about your wife and friends, if you don't mind?"

Sinclair shrugged noncommittally.

"But," he warned in the tone of the bureaucrat that he was, "if you don't follow through with the rehabilitation regimen, you will be given only a short but healthy retirement. Terminal retirement is eighty years of age."

"Yes," Sinclair accepted the political reality of his decision. "Maybe the medicine will help with my energy this year."

"It will make you physically feel better," Vega assured him and then looked at his tablet. "Our time is up. I want you to think about something. You will have something to live for if you have a second career. So we need to explore motivation. You understand? Look at reasons to keep going. Maybe even select a different second career and take another professional aptitude test. You know . . . to see more options."

"Yes," Sinclair agreed, not wishing to delve further into the matter.

"Fortunately," Vega spoke in a cavalier tone, "we are better off today. We have good, constructive options. Just think what people had to face fifty or one hundred years ago."

"What?" Sinclair was caught off guard. His mind had drifted into a brief daydream.

"Like Anna Karenina," Vega explained and laughed. "Look what happened to her."

"Right," Sinclair responded with humor and laughed, too, not giving the allusion a serious thought. Sinclair tried to wipe away the mental cobwebs and to focus on the counselor's words. So far, he felt that the session had been useless and would add to his anxiety. But he decided to keep trying to seek assistance. Maybe Vega was right, and he needed the benefits of the rehabilitation medicine to jump-start his energy level.

"You'll be all right," Vega promised as he stood up to dismiss Sinclair.

Sinclair glanced at the RCA radio and noticed that the clock's hands did not move. "Does it work?" he asked curiously and then pointed at the phone and other objects.

"They all do," Vega revealed proudly. "But I don't play the radio. Vacuum tubes are a rarity, and I couldn't replace them."

They politely shook hands, and the counselor walked around his desk to open the door. "Please," Vega said, placing his hand on Sinclair's shoulder. "Have some confidence. We'll work through this. Your admission today shows real promise and a great first step."

Sinclair nodded politely and watched as the door opened. The counselor warmly tapped his shoulder as he stepped out, and Sinclair heard the door close behind him.

"The same time in two weeks?" a young man confirmed from a reception desk.

"Sure," Sinclair agreed.

He left the building and wondered why he had come in the first place. Only the antiques made the trip worthwhile. Sinclair suddenly wanted to find an old radio after the motorbike was built—maybe even one with an alarm clock. So he put the next counseling session out of his mind and thought instead about options to repair the clamps for his bike's engine. Thinking about his wife's departure helped to cheer him up.

Chapter 5

August 2023
Sanchez

On Fridays, the Social Studies Lab closed in the early afternoon, and the students logged off their tablets to turn them into Sanchez who was the provisional lab supervisor. He counted and logged each tablet, while expecting the students to ask questions about history—any history. Prodding some students to talk about the subject only invited inane requests to visit the bathroom or consult with a counselor. The first week was a short and uneventful experience, offering no new insights into his romantic notion of engaging students about history and stimulating their interest and curiosity. When the last student left, Sanchez sat alone in a room painted to resemble a beach ball with each wall in a different loud color: purple, fuchsia, yellow, lime-green. Throughout the week, he had not known whether he would vomit or suffer an epileptic seizure.

"Pretty ugly?" a familiar voice commented from the far entrance to the long common room at the end of the lab. Sinclair walked into the room and observed Sanchez. He studied the walls and quietly expressed his own revulsion.

"I can't take more of this," Sanchez exclaimed.

Sinclair did not know if he referred to the room or to the lab assignment. "Tough week?" Sinclair probed innocently.

"Boring week," Sanchez countered, making a sweep with his hands. "Tough visual effects."

"I agree," Sinclair said, sitting down on a swivel chair next to him. "I need you to sign this tablet."

He produced his computer and extended it to Sanchez who grasped it tenuously.

"Don't worry," Sinclair tried to dispel his concerns. "It's acknowledging that we had a conference this week." Sanchez skeptically looked up at him.

"Now, please," Sinclair clarified. "I have to submit it today."

Sanchez understood and laughed. "Is this how it all works?" Sanchez challenged this honesty. He quickly signed the tablet and handed it back to Sinclair.

"Oh," Sinclair added shyly. "This is quite ethical. Most of the time mentors don't meet with their teachers."

"I see," Sanchez tried to speak objectively. "Forgotten tradition?"

"Laziness," Sinclair corrected him. "And contempt for the system. Neither teacher nor mentor gives the relationship much validity. It starts with all the good intentions and then dies off slowly. We're too isolated in this job. You felt it this week?"

Sanchez thought about the week and agreed. "Sure did," he expressed his disgust as he pointed at the walls.

"The colors don't help," the mentor agreed and sniggered. Sanchez laughed a bit, too.

"So," Sinclair began to speak again. "Listen. I'll try to get you coverage here. We need university clearance, too."

Silence.

"Then," Sinclair expanded deliberately, "you can teach my course on political science. It is a college-level course. I'll send you an e-mail with the information you need. Textbooks, lesson plans, presentations. Everything. OK?"

"Right," Sanchez perked up contentedly. He didn't tell Sinclair how he had already read and prepared both a lesson plan and lecture. Nor did he tell Sinclair that Pierce had offered some lecture time a week ago.

Sinclair pointed at the walls and laughed again. "It'll give you a brief reprieve from these walls," he joked.

Sanchez beamed happily and took a cursory look at the lab. Then he looked speculatively at Sinclair and wanted to ask, "When?" Sinclair raised his hands to stop him from asking the question.

"Wait," Sinclair warned him. "I need to find coverage. Maybe someone can volunteer. Pierce doesn't want to pay for coverage. But

I Have Three Things to Tell You, My Friend

I can make it happen. Leave it to me as soon as I hear from the college." Sanchez's eyes lit up with hope.

"More than once," Sinclair added as an afterthought. "You need as much exposure as you can get."

"I do!" Sanchez exclaimed.

"Yes," Sinclair agreed and shook his hand. They remained silent for a while, savoring their emotional victory over the walls and the laborious delay of the school's bureaucracy to act on their behalf.

"What do you do when you're not here?" Sanchez inquired seriously.

"What do you mean?"

"Is this all you live for?" he attempted to explain. "Is it enough?"

"Not to be a good teacher," Sinclair blurted out, shocking Sanchez. Sanchez never thought that the teaching profession needed to be supplemented with other activities.

Seeing his confusion, Sinclair amended his explanation. "Let me clear this up," he half-apologized and held up his hand. Sanchez leaned back and patiently waited. Sinclair thought for a while before speaking deliberately about his ideas.

"You see," he began, "if this is all you do—the teaching—then you'll dry up." Sanchez just stared at him. "This job drains you," Sinclair declared simply. "You have to fill it with books, ideas, experiences. Now, with all this virtual school, there is little human interaction. And you have to retreat. Find a refuge to recharge."

"What's your refuge?" Sanchez casually asked.

An apparition of his motorbike and then his wife appeared in his mind, including his readings, historical research, publications, children. Sinclair immediately dismissed the thoughts since he harbored his own doubts.

"You'll find it," he said, "or you won't last." He stood up as if to go.

"I forgot to ask you something," Sanchez persisted. "Can I ask you something personal?"

"Sure," Sinclair answered uneasily.

"What career did you choose for rehabilitation?" Sanchez probed in a frank manner.

A sudden blast of classical music erupted from down the hallway. Sinclair walked curiously to the door and followed the music like a

34

Boy Scout on the trail. When he reached the door, he looked back at Sanchez with a grin.

"Engineering," Sinclair said loudly and walked out into the hallway.

"Engineering?" Sanchez repeated disagreeably. "Not engineering?"

He looked back and saw that Sinclair had stepped into the hallway and walked in the direction of the music. A Mozart concerto played melodically; it took almost no effort to follow Sinclair to the music's source. Sanchez caught a glimpse of Sinclair walking into an open closet at the end of the hallway. Following him, he reached a small chamber where a small, old man dressed in dark blue overalls sat on a stool next to an iPod speaker. He had scant hair on his blotched skull, and through his wire eyeglasses his eyes bulged delightfully upon seeing both men. The white tiled chamber contained a washtub, cleaning supplies, and a spigot hanging over the galvanized tub. Surprisingly, in one corner of the small chamber sat a silver, engraved samovar sitting on a teakwood folding table. The old man instantly offered a cup of tea to Sinclair and looked speculatively at Sanchez who remained in the doorway, just outside the crowded chamber. When Sinclair took the cup, the old man used his free hand to reduce the volume to a barely audible level.

"Welcome," he spoke with a slight Spanish accent. "My . . . friends?"

He gave Sinclair an inquiring look as he took a sip of tea from his own cup. "Excuse me," Sinclair apologized. "I'm mentoring him, sort of. Mr. Sanchez."

"Welcome," the old man repeated. "My name is Smith. Fernando Smith."

Sanchez briefly studied the samovar and looked over at Sinclair.

"Beautiful?" Smith tried to read his mind.

"Absolutely," Sanchez agreed and walked closer to the antique. "Where did you get it?"

"From a friend," Smith pointed to Sinclair as he continued to drink his tea.

"Fantastic," Sanchez commented as he marveled at its artwork. "Russian? Look at all the engraving. Hand-done. Incredibly beautiful."

"No. It's Persian. Old things have their beauty," Smith alluded, as he finished his tea. "What's the use of the pot without good tea leaves?"

He took Sinclair's teacup and his own and placed them both in the tub. The cups, in contrast to the samovar, were old, yellowed plastic mugs.

"Well," the old man stood up, addressing Sinclair. He was shorter than Sanchez and thin with a bony frame. "We must talk, my friend."

Smith made eye contact with Sinclair who immediately understood. "Please excuse us," Sinclair apologized with embarrassment. "I need to speak to Fernando."

"OK," Sanchez felt disappointed. He wanted to ask more questions about the samovar. "Have a good weekend."

"You, too," they almost simultaneously responded.

"Hang in there," Sinclair told him. "Sooner than you think. Have a good Labor Day weekend. Three days off."

"You, too," Sanchez wished them both; he had forgotten about the long weekend.

Sanchez waved good-bye to both of them and walked away. Within a short distance, the music again increased in volume, but he could hear muffled conversations. Smith's angry Spanish accent seemed to eclipse Sinclair's voice, and amid the flow of exquisite music, he heard the old man curse.

"Asshole, I tell you," Smith shouted above the music.

When Sanchez reached the end of the hallway, the voices melted away, and the music along with the argument became a distant din.

September Intermission

Sanchez attended a Labor Day weekend barbeque with Nick at a friend's home. Barbara, who was an attractive middle-aged Hispanic woman, was Nick's surrogate aunt from years past. She and her husband always invited the couple to holiday parties. For some inexplicable reason, Sanchez did not want to attend this Labor Day barbeque. When they arrived, Barbara, wearing a large floral dress, ran up to the two of them and gave them each an exaggerated hug. In tow behind her was a mature black man, wearing an Hawaiian shirt, shorts, and a Dodgers' baseball cap.

"Brandon," she said, "this is my friend, Richard. He was a teacher for forty years and is going into rehabilitation to be a financier. From charity to money, honey."

Richard laughed at her friendly snub and extended his hand to Sanchez and Nick.

"Brandon is a teacher this year," Barbara injected, speaking to Richard.

"Oh," Richard responded cynically. "You ready for the disrespect and neglect? Not like when I started."

Barbara noticed Richard's angst and decided to leave the two alone. "Nick," she said, "let me introduce you to an attorney. An old friend, too. We'll leave these two to talk shop."

Barbara looked over at Richard and Sanchez, who both smiled. She then walked away, and Richard cleared his voice.

"Sorry I came off harshly," Richard apologized. "You want a drink?"

"Later," Sanchez declined. "Thanks."

Richard became awkwardly silent.

"Please tell me what changed," Sanchez said, breaking the silence. "Don't pull any punches." He had a feeling Nick had asked Barbara to find a way to dissuade him from his career choice.

"Voilà," Richard laughed again with a bass voice that attracted the attention of those nearby. "Well, promise not to hit me."

Sanchez gave him a Boy Scout salute and ran his finger across his lips.

"The whole industry is run by experts and software engineers," Richard began to explain. "There is no creativity or ingenuity. Teachers have to follow a regimented curriculum, so students can pass standardized tests. I became a manager when this interface between the students and the standardized curriculum became a reality."

"Right," Sanchez chimed in. "I spent the whole week behind a desk while I supervised students on their computers."

"My point," Richard concurred. "There is no interaction between the student and the provider. In this system, tests, deadlines, and performance are valued. Everything is graded by the computer."

"What about teacher evaluations?" Sanchez followed up.

"Outside experts do them," Richard spoke sadly. "Not even your own supervisors. And the tests evaluate you, too. You have no input in the instruction, but they evaluate you on their virtual performance. How inhuman!"

Sanchez began to wonder if he would ever have a chance to lecture as Sinclair continued his rehabilitation.

"Some dual enrollment classes and AP classes have teacher-student interaction," Sanchez reminded Richard.

"Rare," Richard clarified. "It's only a small percentage of the best. The rest are regimented through digital pabulum. It's not for me. I feel sorry for the kids."

Sanchez began to feel regret. "What do you miss from the old days?" he asked.

"Simple. Life. Conversations. Dialogue. Human interaction," Richard spelled it out as he took one long gulp of his drink. "I miss the unpredictability of teaching. Everything is too predictable."

"That's why you like finance?" Sanchez joked.

Richard looked down and took another drink. "Exactly," Richard confirmed. "It is so much more unpredictable than teaching. Teaching has been reduced to ID numbers and the judgment of faceless experts. And these experts have never taught. No other profession has outsiders calling the shots. Maybe plumbers should be on medical boards? The educators been taken out of it. There's no joy in it anymore."

"What joy?" Barbara's voice could be heard from behind.

Sanchez turned to see her and Nick, holding out two drinks.

"Here." Nick gave Sanchez one of them. "It's hot." Sanchez took the drink immediately to his lips.

"Did Richard reveal to you the belly of the beast?" she asked and snickered at her joke.

Sanchez was silent as Nick and Barbara exchanged glances.

"I told him the ups and downs," Richard said. "He'll survive. We all do. Teachers are a tough lot."

"Richard told me what I already had seen this week," Sanchez said, trying to dampen the shock of the revelation. "Good to meet you," he said to the older man. They shook hands.

"Let's go meet everyone else," Barbara said, pulling Sanchez away. "Talking shop can be such a bore during holidays. Why call it Labor Day? We have no need to labor over our conversations." Barbara again laughed, and everyone politely joined her.

Sanchez, like a good guest, obediently followed his hostess along with Nick, leaving Richard to gravitate towards some other guests.

"Don't take it so hard," Richard threw out one last idea. "Maybe the computers will all crash and burn." He hooted and turned around to face the other guests who searched to understand what was so funny. They had enough liquor in their system to make any joke palatable. As for Sanchez, he spent the rest of the evening, drowning in the fog of an alcoholic binge until his internal computer crashed.

———

When Sinclair dropped off his wife, he felt good. His day was going well. The clamps had been repaired on his motorbike the day before. With his wife leaving for an exchange program in Japan, he had some of the proverbial space he needed to think and consider some important decisions in the month ahead. At the Bradley Terminal, he had a flashback when Rachel passed through the TSA security gate.

Sinclair recalled Sophie, who had French-kissed him before boarding a return flight to Sao Pablo. He had proposed marriage to her, but she sadly declined. She did not want to remain in Los Angeles. It was 1984, and sadly, like their relationship, the Olympics had ended. The terminal seemed empty in the midafternoon. Apologizing for not staying, she invited him to visit her in Brazil. She explained she could never leave her home or family. Then, the postcard arrived. She was engaged to be married, and this circumstance forced his options to zero. Once decisions were made, they were sometimes irreversible, especially when they were made too late. Sinclair played out the last few moments that he saw Sophie disappear into the passageway—never to return. When Rachel disappeared behind the security barrier, he turned around and went home alone as he did thirty years ago. He never expected Rachel to disappear, too, although he could pretend that would happen.

Chapter 6

October 2023
Sanchez

"Two. Ah . . . two . . ."
—Fernando Smith (The Janitor)

Sanchez sat in a dismal yellow room located in a nondescript building. A student who chose education as a major would rarely need to pass through the main thoroughfare of the campus and rub shoulders with the popular engineering and business undergraduates. Like many California universities, the institution had undergone several transformations and construction surges after the Second World War, when veterans earned an inexpensive postsecondary education. At first, the education building held a noble place among the assortment of science, humanities, arts, and engineering buildings

After the 1960s, when the teaching profession began to lose its luster, the education department remained in its location, while other departments either moved to better campus locations or received a facelift. Soon, it began to share its space with other departments in decline, like psychology, English, and political science. Before the turn of the 21st century, the new administration relocated the education department to the far end of the campus, where it was housed in a converted brick building, once used for classrooms in miscellaneous courses and equipment storage. For the last twenty years, the department, like a poor relation, inherited used and obsolete equipment from other departments.

Sanchez unfortunately sat in a mandatory adolescent health class in the dilapidated education building. The classroom had recently been issued a used Smart Board and Wi-Fi upgrade. It was a technological decade behind state-of-the-art equipment. After the first five weeks, the Smart Board failed, and the midterm test had to be issued in a paper format—an unheard of event in any other department. This inconvenience, among others, exasperated Sanchez.

He sat in his favorite location near the door, so he could slip out of the room when the professor looked the other way. Escaping into the hallway was not difficult since the professor spent his lecture eyeing the prettiest female students who sat on the opposite side of the room. Since the unreliable Wi-Fi occasionally crippled his Internet access, Sanchez and his classmates became their professor's captive audience. They were obligated to listen to his three-hour lecture filled with rambling digressions.

Standing exactly five feet tall, Professor Kylp had entered his rehabilitation year and decided to spend his lecture time on personal musings, rarely lecturing on the course material. He looked like a mad scientist, wearing a faded black blazer over a starched white shirt and black, polyester trousers. His black shoes appeared to be orthopedic and shined with old layers of waxy polish. When he lectured, he swayed from side to side and walked around a pencil style podium.

Sanchez regretted not taking the course in a virtual classroom. Since misery loved company, he found an equally miserable classmate, Liz, who vocally shared her disgust with the course and the professor. She was Sanchez's age and had accepted an educational post instead of her real interest, computer programming. Sadly, she had been placed on the waiting list.

She had dark eyes and complexion and dressed fashionably. Sanchez would have asked her out if he were not gay, which ironically worked in his favor.

"Did he start?" Liz asked, looking away from Sanchez.

"He's not even here," Sanchez delightedly told her.

No one liked Kylp. He surveyed the room and noticed that it had fewer students than the last class. Counting the students present, Sanchez estimated that fifty percent were missing. 'Lucky them,' he thought.

"Did you read the material?" she asked. Liz had a strong disdain for the reading material. In her opinion, it bordered on the absurd.

"Sure," he assured her. "The lectures have nothing to do with the test. Do I have a choice?"

Liz sighed, and looking through her bag, she produced her small tablet. "I summarized the notes," she told Sanchez. "But there is too much info to remember."

"Right," Sanchez agreed. "I can never figure out what will or will not be on the test."

Liz began to click the keys on her tablet and study her notes. "This time it's about sex," she spoke with exasperation. "I didn't know teenagers' sex lives were so complicated."

"It was soooo long ago," Sanchez responded sarcastically.

Liz giggled. "Ages," she returned. Scrolling through the tablet, she stopped to make a comment. "Did you read about this?" Liz held up the tablet for Sanchez to read. "It's perverse!"

Sanchez, amused, glanced over to read, but Liz snatched it away. "Shit," she cursed, as she noticed Kylp enter the room with a half ream of multiple-choice tests and two dozen pencils in his grip.

"Did you see that?" Liz raised her voice in shock. "He brought pencils? What gives?"

"Better than a fountain pen and ink wells," Sanchez retorted. They chuckled.

"I can't believe this," Liz said in disappointment and returned her attention to her tablet.

A moment later, an old man, dressed in old blue jeans, sneakers, and a green-checkered shirt, strutted into the classroom and stood behind the professor who arranged the tests and pencils on the small podium. Precariously balanced, they managed to stay on top of the podium. The professor made instant eye contact and turned away.

The old man, a guest lecturer, carried a leather mailbag that closely hugged his hip. He tightly grasped the bag and confidently scanned the room, fixing his eyes on the same coeds that Kylp liked to ogle.

"Who in the hell is he?" Liz questioned.

"Hell is right," Sanchez agreed. "This has to be good if he is here to talk about teenage sex."

"I hope he's not a pedophile," Liz bemoaned and turned her attention to her tablet.

A loud clamor of chatter began to escalate, and Kylp exchanged a confidential word with his guest. Facing the class, he called the students to order. "Let me introduce my guest," he began. "Actually my guest and my friend." The clamor immediately settled into a tolerable undertone of reserved conversations.

"This is Mark," Kylp introduced his guest. Mark smiled and fastened his attention on the coeds. "He's here to talk about the social ramifications of sexually transmitted diseases among teenagers," he continued his introduction. "Mark?"

Mark stepped forward. A gentle applause welcomed him. "Hello," he saluted the class with a wave. "Thank you for having me here today." Silence descended on the class.

"I got involved with booze when I was in high school. It caused me to fuck up my life royally!" Mark blurted out. "Then I ended up in jail many times. Now I have a problem with my rehabilitation petition. I might not get a second chance to make it good."

He paused to gather himself while he wiped his eyes. Kylp kindly tapped his shoulder, and everyone waited sympathetically.

"Is he on probation?" Liz whispered.

"Looks like it," Sanchez assumed.

"OK," Mark continued to speak. "The drugs and alcohol made me a sinner. I was straight when I went to prison. They made me suck cock. I was raped. I thought I liked it for a long time. I told myself to like it. I thought I was gay until the Twelve Steps saved me . . ."

"Who invited this crazy homophobe?" Liz angrily spoke aloud. No one heard her amid the explosion of supportive and antagonistic remarks from the class. "I thought the topic was about teenage sex," Liz shouted into Sanchez's ear.

Sanchez motioned for her to follow him into the hallway. Liz stepped out of the classroom as the shouting began to die down.

"I don't want to hurt anyone's feelings," Mark apologized. "I want to show you how alcohol and drugs hurt me. There's nothing wrong with being gay, but I wasn't gay. You see the alcohol did it . . ."

Liz and Sanchez could hear his rambling monologue digress about the horrors of prison rape. This time he provided gratuitous details. "He made me swallow," Mark declared. "I liked it because I liked drugs."

"Oh shit," Sanchez cursed.

"He's crazy," Liz said.

"Kylp's an asshole to invite him," Sanchez added.

"We've got to do something," Liz said. She felt the bias of Mark's speech crushing her sense of propriety. "I won't take this."

"Let's go to the dean," Sanchez announced firmly.

"The dean?" Liz objected. "Now?"

Determined, Sanchez walked off.

Liz followed him out of the building, and they crossed the campus grounds to the Humanities Department. Scores of students were moving across the grounds while entering and leaving other buildings. Sanchez and Liz were able to navigate their way directly towards the building. Soon they reached the dean's office on the second floor. A small vestibule separated it from the hallway where the other administrators worked. Convinced of the justice of his action, Sanchez raced ahead.

"This is it," he said.

Liz followed him inside the vestibule where a mature secretary sat behind a gray polymer desk. "We're here to speak to the dean," Liz spoke in an outraged tone. "This matter has to be addressed immediately."

The secretary expressed skepticism. "It's bad," Sanchez righteously declared. "We're teachers, and there is a guest lecturer who is a homophobe in our health class. He's talking about someone forcing him to swallow semen in prison."

The secretary's eyes popped open, and her composure changed from skepticism to disgust.

"Oh! How awful!" the secretary uttered distastefully, standing up. "Let me see." She paused before entering the dean's office. "The class is in session now?" she asked.

"Right now!" Liz spoke in a shrill voice.

"Yes," the secretary turned around, knocked and entered the dean's office.

From inside, the conversation, somewhat muted, seeped through the glass door. Liz and Sanchez waited by the secretary's desk. Occasionally, Sanchez would look at his smart watch for the time and for messages.

"They should be on break soon," he reminded Liz. "Then there's the quiz." Liz nodded, understanding their time was limited. "I just got to say what is on my mind," he complained. "I can't take it anymore."

"Let's hope the dean talks to us," she said optimistically.

The homophobic words did not bother Sanchez as much as the sheer ignorance and uncouth tone. He was thick-skinned about insults aimed against gays. On the other hand, Kylp and Mark had crossed the line when they treated the class like a workshop for recovering addicts and sexual deviants.

The secretary meekly stepped out of the office. "The dean is aware of the situation," the secretary noted.

"How?" Liz screeched brashly.

"We didn't give you the professor's name," Sanchez retorted angrily.

"It's the only education health class at this hour," the secretary explained calmly. "This isn't the first time we heard about some controversy concerning Professor Kylp."

Her previous expression of shock had melted away, and implacable stubbornness took hold. "The professor's free speech is protected," she reminded them.

"But its offensive," Liz countered, edging towards the dean's office door.

"You can't see her now," the secretary warned her. "But you have your rights." Liz and Sanchez paused to grasp her meaning.

"The dean wants you to file a complaint," the secretary advised. "It must be submitted by tomorrow morning with other petitions and complaints you may collect. She will address the issue with the professor and contact you within the week. It's all stipulated in the student handbook. I suggest you read it."

"Right," Liz said despondently.

"Good old handbook," Sanchez concluded cynically.

"Yes," the secretary confirmed. "On the form tab in section six. Do you have any questions?"

"No," he said. Sanchez felt like crying. He wanted to hit something. "Except that the guest can be obnoxious with no consequences? He's not in the handbook."

"He's a guest under the protection of academic freedom," the secretary reminded them. "It needs to be investigated. That's all there is."

"I'm confident it will be investigated," Liz responded sarcastically and followed Sanchez into the hallway. "Since it's his last year before rehabilitation."

Sanchez opened the door and stepped out. Liz followed.

"Have a good evening," the secretary wished them with a saccharine smile.

"You, too, bitch," Liz shouted and slammed the door.

Sanchez stared at her and wondered why he did not say the same thing.

"I'm sure they will love reading our complaint later," he wisecracked. "After you told her to fuck herself."

"I didn't say fuck," she countered.

"Close," he argued. "Bitch isn't exactly a nice word."

"It is a female dog."

"Woof."

She glared at him for a second and then burst out laughing. "Fuck it," she yelled. "I'll send them the biggest complaint they've ever seen."

"From both of us," he added proudly. "Then they will use it as toilet paper."

"Ah," she chortled and walked back to class.

Students continued to enter and exit other buildings. The education building appeared abandoned.

"I love seeing that we're a select and privileged minority," Sanchez said pessimistically.

"Yes. The privileged and abused," Liz added, "and alone."

"I miss the old days," he commented as they entered the building.

"Why?" she asked, curious.

Sanchez stopped and looked directly at her. "Because we can't quit," he explained, "and sign up for a new major."

"This whole rehabilitation thing isn't working for young people," she sadly observed. "Is it?"

"It sucks," he exclaimed and continued to walk towards the classroom.

"Some old definitions still work," she agreed, catching up to Sanchez. "I like suck."

"Me, too," he approved.

They simultaneously stopped and laughed together.

"There they go!" she declared.

The students sulked as they filed into the classroom.

"Here it comes," he forewarned. "The useless test!"

"Ah," Liz uttered in frustration, carefully looking around. "The creep is gone, I think. But the prof will still have a bunch of inane questions on the test. "

"It can't beat the one about marijuana and homosexuality on the last test," he pointed out.

"I told you he's a homophobe!" she repeated resentfully.

Sanchez and Liz joined the other students as they settled into their seats.

"He's gone," he confirmed.

"But the professor is still here," she retorted in disappointment.

"One out of two ain't bad," he joked.

Liz ignored him for the moment as one of the privileged coeds distributed pencils and another distributed the test packets. "Real high tech," she commented.

Liz held up the pencil and stuck it into the middle of her closed fist to make an obscene gesture.

"Good," Sanchez snickered.

The coeds quickly finished distributing the tests

"OK," Kylp called for attention. "When you finish the test, turn it in and sign the attendance form."

"Can't wait," Liz spoke under her breath.

"Begin," Kylp ordered.

He looked around the room and then down at his tablet.

Sanchez looked over at Liz, who shrugged and began to answer the questions. He bubbled in the answers with alacrity until he skipped ahead and jumped to the bottom page. Rereading one question several times, he stopped and called Liz's attention to it.

She slowly noticed his gesture.

Pointing to the bottom of the second page, Sanchez directed her to look at the last question on the page. Liz turned over the page and read it carefully.

"Oh,my God!" she barked and then giggled.

The class stopped to look at her as Sanchez stood up to leave the classroom.

"I got to go," she excused herself as Kylp looked up from his tablet.

They left their tests on their desks. Liz darted out of the room and met Sanchez at the end of the hallway.

"I can't believe it!" she called out to him.

He stopped in front of a restroom and began to hoot loudly.

"Where are you going?" she managed to spit out as she laughed, too.

"To check out the question!" Sanchez explained.

His explanation caused her to bellow even more.

"Well?" she forced herself to ask. "You let me know what direction a man's erection leans. To the right or to the left?"

"Coming right up," Sanchez jested.

Looking scornfully down at his crotch, he dramatically tapped his forehead as if he were pondering a deep problem. He then held up his forefinger and moved it to the right and then to the left.

"The world waits," he dramatically declared in a pompous tone and opened the restroom door. "Such questions need to be solved for science!"

"You need my help?" she coquettishly offered.

"This is a job for a lone homosexual," he declined and entered the restroom.

Inside, Sanchez could hear Liz chuckling loudly.

They soon had their answer but decided to leave the test question unanswered to remain a mystery for humanity.

Chapter 7

October 2023
Sinclair

As scheduled on the school calendar, Sinclair's Free Speech Club met in his Social Science Lab every Tuesday after school hours. Luckily, the club avoided the budget chopping block after fiscal restraints threatened its existence. Despite the financial challenges, the Free Speech Club had the second highest attendance after the Key Club. Unlike the other clubs, its membership—except for the hardcore members—vacillated. Although the roster officially registered sixty members, some meetings entertained twenty to one hundred students at a time.

Sinclair watched as the students entered his lab in groups of five and ten. The room housed fifty lab students, but on this day attendance climbed over seventy. Obviously, many were nonmembers, and this began to concern Sinclair. George, the vice president, roamed among the students to swap jokes and to share gossip with members and nonmembers alike. He purposely avoided speaking to Sinclair. Something was amiss. Asma, the president, was absent. She had lobbied the administration for the creation of the club, despite objections from the activities director, Chris Stile, a fanatical evangelical. The meeting was already ten minutes late in starting.

"Mr. Sinclair," a tenth-grade girl dressed in a gray blouse and black uniform pants, called. "Where's Asma?"

"She's coming," Sinclair hoped.

The club was Asma's "baby," and she would never miss a meeting. Sinclair knew from last year that Asma's tardiness usually hinted at some controversy or brewing crisis. He feared that an encounter with an administrator might have stymied Asma. George wandered next to Sinclair's desk, as he earnestly read a text message on his smart watch.

"Asma," he announced, shoving the tiny screen in front of Sinclair's face, "said to go outside."

"Great," Sinclair said with dread.

Bad news waited.

After pushing through the meandering squads of students and stepping over some who squatted on the carpeted floor, Sinclair managed to push his way towards the lab's exit door.

"She's outside, Mr. Sinclair," the tenth-grade girl happily told him. "I saw her."

"Thanks," he answered.

Even though the lab bustled with loud conversations and laughs, Sinclair could hear Asma's squealing voice, but he did not understand her exact words.

She sounded upset.

George followed at his heels and quickly stood next to Asma, who was in the middle of an animated conversation with a junior and senior club member. She stopped her ranting and dismissed her companions with a shrug of her shoulder.

"We have to talk," she demanded instantly.

Sinclair remained silent, remembering the script Asma liked to play out when she believed the club was in a crisis.

"George," she ordered her vice president, "start the discussions. Can you have Bret and Jessie help you lead them?"

George looked at Sinclair to protest, but he immediately surrendered. He succumbed to Asma's threatening body language.

Ironically, Asma, a first-generation Somali-American, posed no physical threat to anyone. She stood less than five feet tall and was so thin that a casual observer might have thought that she was anorexic. Her dark complexion and pitch-black eyes seemed to highlight her petite stature. But, in spite of her diminutive height, she carried the presence of Atlas. Asma's forceful will and strong opinions dominated her environment. She was a woolly mammoth violently stuffed into the body of a black flamingo—crushing the meek, weak, and confused.

"Yeah," George agreed forlornly and led the other students back to the lab.

"Where can we talk?" Asma asked politely, offering a congenial smile.

It failed to disguise her rage.

"The usual," Sinclair told her.

She abruptly turned around and walked towards the janitor's closet at the end of the hallway.

Sinclair remained silent and smiled at the students who were watching them.

"I'll be back in five minutes," Asma repeated. "George will start off. Go ahead."

The club members reluctantly turned around and entered the lab, expressing their dissatisfaction that George would be leading the club meeting. Sinclair kept his own counsel and prepared himself for Asma's verbal onslaught.

They entered the open closet and left the door open.

"Go ahead," Sinclair invited her.

Asma attempted to speak and then stopped. She listened for George's voice to start the meeting.

"This is really bad," Asma said.

"Go ahead," Sinclair encouraged, bracing himself for the firestorm.

He did not want this aggravation at the end of his career.

Asma looked at him in disappointment for a moment and took a deep breath as she tried to subdue some of her volatility.

"They won't fund us," she stated and huffed in displeasure.

"Who?" he demanded to know.

"Everyone," she spoke with frustration.

She had a tendency to refer to people as abstractions.

"Good," Sinclair sarcastically answered. "Now I can ask everyone on the staff!"

"Ah," Asma groaned. "You know!"

A few students peeked into the closet. Asma crossly glared at them, and they scurried away.

George could be heard having a heated exchange with a student.

"He's not doing too well," Sinclair commented.

"You got to go," Asma ignored him. "Please."

"You didn't tell me who," he reminded her.

"You know," she repeated. "Stile!"

Sinclair took a deep breath.

"Listen," he carefully explained. "I told you that Pierce approved the budget."

"But I am the president, and we had a meeting last period," Asma clarified her position. "The one with club presidents?"

"OK," Sinclair wanted her to make her point.

"He told me that Pierce may pull the funds," Asma raised her voice. "This may be the last meeting."

"Let me see," Sinclair promised and walked off. He hoped Pierce was in his office.

"You're going to talk to Mr. Stile?" Asma questioned, following him into the hallway.

"Pierce," Sinclair stopped to explain. "Stile is a waste of time."

"Tell me about it," Asma confirmed. "Just like the crazies in my family."

She watched him walk away and halted to listen to the contentious words George and several students were exchanging over the topic of transgendered adoptions and Judeo-Christian beliefs.

Sinclair ignored the debate and continued walking to Pierce's office. Unlike other administrators, Pierce stayed after school, and Sinclair thought he had a reasonable chance of speaking with the man before he went home. When he reached the office, the door was slightly ajar. He could hear a muted conversation transpiring inside. The secretary had gone home, so he quietly approached the door and knocked.

"Come in," Pierce welcomed the unseen visitor.

The room became silent.

Sinclair walked in and saw Stile sitting in front of Pierce and holding his tablet. The man wore an expensive Italian suit and a tacky bow tie. The suit failed to disguise his corpulent body. Stile resembled a cartoon caricature, mixing Fred Flintstone with Boris Badenov. He spoke in a high-pitched voice that shrieked like an eagle with laryngitis, and he had a volatile personality and the talent to exploit his screeching histrionics. Sinclair could never figure out which assistant superintendent had been bribed to shield Stile from a lawsuit or dismissal.

Noticing the active Smart Board behind Pierce, Sinclair intensely studied the school budget and a list of extracurricular activities. He quickly discovered that his club had been highlighted along with a few others.

"I know why you are here," Pierce spoke defensively. "Please sit down."

Stile ignored him, but Sinclair sat down next to him. Pierce tried to appear conciliatory and pointed to the Smart Board.

"I have a reduction of state funds this year," he bluntly stated.

"Yes," Sinclair agreed but did not want to give Stile the upper hand. "My club has the highest membership. Other clubs are losing members, and some have only a handful of kids."

"Yes," Pierce agreed reluctantly.

He remained silent, and Sinclair continued to take the initiative.

Sinclair pointed his finger at Stile, while Stile fumed. "He . . ." Sinclair began.

Pierce uncomfortably straightened himself in his chair and resigned himself to listen to Sinclair's fusillade of recriminations.

Pierce reminded Stile to remain calm.

Stile twitched in his seat but remained silent. Knowing Pierce, Sinclair was sure that he had coached Stile. But he also knew that the man could not maintain his composure for long.

"He's sabotaging the club for his own agenda," Sinclair finished his thoughts.

"Excuse me?" Pierce expressed offense at the accusation.

"He called it the devil's club," Sinclair quickly added, "at a Priority Club meeting last year."

"Mr. Sinclair!" Pierce objected.

Stile smiled widely and held up his hand. Pierce politely acquiesced with a welcoming gesture.

"Sir?" Stile sought permission. "Please?"

Pierce nodded.

Sinclair began to count to ten.

"I have no bias against Mr. Sinclair's club," Stile spoke calmly and smiled at Sinclair. "The gentleman is just listening to a few very incorrigible students."

"Incorrigible?" Sinclair questioned openly. "What about the recording . . ."

"Mr. Sinclair," Pierce interrupted him. "Mr. Stile apologized about that incident."

"He did," Sinclair concurred. "Under duress! He was going to lose his position. You can't go around, as he did, and say that no godless club will ever be organized on his campus. I am surprised he is still here. This is a free speech class, and the students have a constitutional right to criticize anything. Even religion. We have students of every belief and nonbelief."

Stile began to fidget, and his smile melted into a frown.

"We know the history," Pierce changed the subject. "But I have a budget. Rules and stipulations. Fiscal obligations."

"I understand that the bylaws rule out closing a large club," Sinclair reminded Pierce, "unless that club is in some violation of a regulation. There must be a valid reason."

Sinclair stopped speaking and looked at both men.

Pierce made eye contact with Stile, but he maintained a poker face. Stile's face reddened, and he instantly looked down on his tablet.

"Well," Pierce spoke with measured words. "This year the club is funded."

"Yes," Sinclair concurred. "But I am asking about next year."

Stile kept his head down.

"Next year," Pierce clarified, "you will be in rehabilitation. I will be reassigned most likely. And the club budget could be restored. Let's leave it as it is."

Sinclair, not wanting to stay for another moment, stood up and walked to the door.

"I have to get back to my club's meeting," he informed them.

Pierce smiled affably.

"Thank you, Mr. Sinclair," he said. "How is Mr. Sanchez doing?"

"Great," Sinclair complimented his prodigy. "He'll be an excellent teacher. I am scheduling him as a guest lecturer."

"Good," he reacted with happiness. "We need excellent teachers for the future. Don't forget you need the university to clear his paperwork."

Stile smiled to himself and continued to look down at his tablet, as he scrolled through the screen.

"OK," Sinclair acknowledged. "I want Mr. Sanchez to be the club sponsor next year. I thought I'd give Mr. Stile a heads-up on that one since you and I won't be here next year."

Stile slightly raised his head to respond, but he stopped. He continued to avert his eyes.

"Have a good day," Pierce dismissed him.

Sinclair walked out of the room. Halfway down the hall, he heard Pierce's door close, and he thought he heard Stile begin to carp like a preschooler.

October Intermission

Smith, in his royal blue uniform, cap, and safety shoes, showed up at work early, making sure he avoided the other janitors. He wanted to confront Rubio, his boss, who had promised to submit his rehabilitation forms before the deadline. After Smith had spoken to Sinclair and another union representative, Rubio received a notice reminding him of his legal obligation and pointing out the severity of neglecting it. He responded and promised, both verbally and in writing, to submit the documents as required in his official role as a supervisor. Checking with the rehabilitation office and his account online, Smith discovered that the document was still missing. Later the rehabilitation office assured him that there was a delay between submission and the recording of the document. He had time.

Relax.

Smith mistrusted both the office and Rubio. He had an inner feeling that Rubio was legally postponing the process to torture him.

Rubio was a sadist.

With dread, Smith wandered across the campus and stopped by Rubio's empty office. The man was apparently absent. Smith reluctantly backtracked to the office of Rubio's assistant, Kiki, to pick up his biometric precoded keys. Her door was open.

"You see Rubio?" Smith demanded to know, as he waited impatiently for her to give him his keys.

Kiki was a voluptuous black woman, who resented Rubio with as much antipathy as Smith. Once Rubio had propositioned Kiki, but she did not file a sexual harassment complaint. Instead, she threatened her boss with a broken broomstick. The threat was enough to dissuade Rubio from trying to unbutton her blouse again.

A mutual abhorrence of Rubio was all that Smith and she shared, however. Smith had an aversion to Kiki, not because she was an African-American, but because she did not measure up to his standards for a woman. Her churlish behavior upset him for he had been raised to appreciate vocally submissive and physically passive women. Besides, she had openly invited him to join her and another female janitor, a mildly handicapped woman with a slight limp, for a drink at a strip joint. The invitation was still open.

"Smithy," Kiki said, ignoring his question. "You are looking hot tonight!" Kiki licked her red lips and cast a desirous eye on him

"I need to talk to the son of a bitch," Smith warned her.

"Well," Kiki spoke in disappointment. "I'd best forget partying with you later. You'll probably end up in jail if you see Rubio."

"He has my paperwork!" Smith reminded her.

"He's out," Kiki said, satisfying his inquiry. "I'm in charge."

Kiki leaned back and looked for his keys. Finding them, she handed the keys to him along with a bar of chocolate.

"It's the same thing every night," she told him sullenly. "Every night. You need to chill. He has to submit the paperwork. It's the law. Listen, you got the fucker by the balls."

"Puto," Smith cursed and took the keys. "Where is he?"

He opened the chocolate bar and took a bite.

"Don't know," Kiki admitted. "He called, saying he's not coming in."

Smith looked skeptically at her.

"Really," she pleaded, holding up her hands. "No más. I don't know any more."

"Gracias," he thanked her.

"You're welcome," Kiki said, cheering up enough to add, "good looking!"

Smith ignored the compliment. She laughed.

"I will bring you my country's chocolate to you one day," he promised. "Tell him I need to talk to him."

"Where's Helen?" Smith asked about a female janitor he liked.

No one knew. But Kiki suspected. "You mean Cinderella?" she teased him.

Smith blushed and ignored her allusion.

"I don't know fucking Cinderella," he irritatingly rejected the nickname.

Kiki decided to change the subject. "Rubio will avoid you, hombre," Kiki chided him. "You know that. Unless I come along. And I won't. I have enough shit on my plate. You know what I mean?"

"Why?" Smith stopped eating his chocolate. He felt slighted.

Kiki paused to study his perplexed expression. "I might kill him with you," Kiki confided. "That bastard lives because he's the boss. I need my job. Got to pay the bills. I need to get a boob job." Kiki cupped her breasts with her hands and mockingly pushed them forward. She chuckled at her joke.

"Ah," Smith said embarrassed. "You can keep your tits."

"I'm joking," Kiki assured him. "I really don't want to kill him.'

"Leave it to me," Smith assured her. "I am the hombre. The man."

Smith raised his remaining piece of chocolate bar to her and walked out of Kiki's office.

Kiki watched him uneasily for a moment and snickered. In her mind, Smith was an odd, but silly old man.

"That fucker. Love him," Kiki mumbled to herself. "He is so wicked. Rubio better watch out." One day, she thought, she would feed him more than a chocolate bar. Fernando needed to loosen up. She looked down at her breasts and laughed.

Sinclair added the cables and brakes to his motorbike, but when he tried to install the spark plug, he discovered a problem. The refurbishment company had sent him the wrong size. Memorizing the spark's spec measurements, Sinclair left his garage and walked to his office to search for a replacement online. He sent an e-mail to the motorbike company and then scanned through his messages. He had received a few from his wife. They contained only bland platitudes and colorless descriptions of her experiences in Japan. Reading her messages, he recalled another place he had once wished to visit.

On an impulse, Sinclair looked up the country of Brazil and began to search for the places Sophie had described to him decades ago. The last month had brought changes. The rehabilitation shots had renewed forgotten feelings and memories. These dormant urges surged through his mind and body, as he recalled Sophie's description of Fernando de Noronha. The beautiful archipelago of islands in Brazil contained pristine beaches, exotic landscapes and wildlife. Sophie had told him that, when she had dived in the area, the clarity of the water reached down to depths of fifty feet.

Looking through the online tourist videos, Sinclair succumbed to his nostalgia and took a local virtual tour of the region. He followed the guide across the white sands and into the blue-green waters to plunge into the sea where sea turtles, dolphins, sharks, and a wide range of colorful fish swam. Eyes closed, he imagined an underwater excursion with Sophie in the waters below and above on the beach as he tried to recapture her words, gestures, and presence. As with all unfulfilled desires, his attempt to relive a nonexistent past left him feeling incomplete. The power of the rehabilitation shots magnified the pain of his loss when he opened his eyes. All he had left was an absent wife, a disintegrating career, and a bleak unknown future. He needed to decide, or he would die before his actual death. A new career would not be enough of a cure for an unhappy life.

Fortunately, his wallowing in regret and pity was short-lived. Smith had sent him an angry e-mail complaining about Rubio. He had already sent him a dozen irate messages throughout the week.

Maybe Sinclair was not so fortunate.

Chapter 8

November 2023
Sanchez

"Two—A long and painful death"
—Fernando Smith (The Janitor)

When Sanchez arrived at the gym, a gaggle of students, behaving in the secondary school mode of controlled chaos, milled about, shouted, coerced, cursed, and struggled to complete their clubs' floats for the Saturday homecoming game. Every club proudly displayed their motifs in bold exhibitions of color, using both creative posters and electronic devices. LED message boards exposed phrases and images in keeping with the homecoming theme. A few clubs used a collage of paper-thin monitors to create running images that advertised club events, past and future, along with achievements and histories. All of the homecoming floats sat on their power source, modified lithium battery carts that had been submerged inside the decorative creations. The members had been working on the floats since the beginning of the year.

As he walked around the gym, Sanchez perused the clubs' floats, categorized by the different activities they represented: ethnic groups, sports, charities, and honor societies. In many ways, the assemblage looked like a cross between a world's fair and a UN convention. Multiple languages could be heard, subordinate within phrases of English. The students' energy carried Sanchez unconsciously through the miasma of frantic efforts. A loud, booming voice stopped him in his tracks.

"Sanchez!" Sinclair shouted several times. "Come here."

I Have Three Things to Tell You, My Friend

Sanchez looked to his right and saw a simple float with a large collage of screens. Images flashed in synchrony, and variations were subtitled with verbal pronouncements. Occasionally the center screen showed a fragmented video, while the peripheral screens presented colorful subjects of natural scenery.

"Welcome to the Free Speech Club," Sinclair said proudly.

On the float's center screen, an animated video showed Robert Ingersoll speaking to a 19th century American audience. He was a tall, portly, bald white man, wearing an impeccable cravat that matched his affable face and the twinkle of his sardonic eyes:

It is a thousand times better to have common sense without education than to have education without common sense.

"He was a Victorian rock star," a female voice happily announced behind Sanchez.

He turned around and saw Asma holding a flexible monochrome screen in her hand.

"We got more quotes," she said, clicking a key on her tablet. "Check it out."

Flashing on the screens were various quotes, appearing and disappearing, along with their attributions:

"The absurd is the essential concept and the first truth."
—Albert Camus

"Men are from Earth, women are from Earth. Deal with it."
—George Carlin

"Human decency is not derived from religion. It precedes it."
—Christopher Hitchens

"Remember your humanity, and forget the rest."
—Bertrand Russell

"You can spend your life judging people or, you can spend it making friends. Take your pick."
—Carroll Bryant

"Cool?" Asma asked proudly.

Her smile instantly vanished as she looked up at a flashing quote from the Priority Club's float:

"An atheist is one who hopes the Lord will do nothing to disturb his disbelief."
—Franklin P. Jones

"They just copied from us," Asma complained. "We thought it up first."

She began to walk up to the float, and Sinclair stopped her in time before a dispute ensued.

"We can't draw any unnecessary attention," Sinclair warned her. He pointed to the left of the float, where Stile was staring disapprovingly at the Free Speech Club's quotes. "He's looking for an excuse," Sinclair reminded her.

Stile turned to speak to a member of the Priority Club.

"He won't come here," Sinclair assured her.

Stile gave a withering glance at Asma and Sinclair and strolled off to visit another club's float.

"He pisses me off," Asma declared and stormed away. She suddenly stopped and turned around. "What did he say about the funding?"

Sinclair raised his finger to his lips, and she responded with an icy smile. The other club members were watching. When nothing more was said, they returned to their work; they did not wish to listen to their president's tirade. They felt reassured that Sinclair could assuage her anger.

"You didn't say hello to Mr. Sanchez," Sinclair pointed out. "He's your new sponsor next year. You got to break him in."

Sinclair clapped Sanchez on the back and smiled at Asma. The introduction made Sanchez uneasy.

"I'm sorry," she apologized but ignored Sanchez. "Why do you have to retire?"

Sinclair became annoyed at her obstinacy, but he tried to maintain an atmosphere of cordiality for Sanchez's sake.

"We talked about this," Sinclair reminded her with a stern look. "Enough. Let's make Mr. Sanchez welcome."

Everyone just stared.

"Welcome," Asma said, adopting her political persona. "Since Mr. Sinclair recommends you, I guess I should be glad you'll be here next year."

"I don't know . . ." Sanchez began, trying to distance himself from the commitment.

Sanchez did not know if he would remain at the school at the end of the year or be accepted at law school. So he did not wish to be drawn into a family argument.

"Of course, you will," Sinclair stymied his objections. "You'll get a raving review from me and the kids."

Asma, still upset, gave Sinclair an impromptu hug.

"We'll miss you, Mr. Sinclair," she told him sadly.

An ovation of "Ah" resounded from the club members.

"OK," Sinclair said and pointed to the float as she broke away. "Nothing like the present. We have to make up time."

Sinclair then touched Sanchez's elbow and escorted him closer to the float.

"They've been working on this since last month," Sinclair noted proudly.

"Since August," Asma corrected him.

"Right," Sinclair agreed confusingly.

A few of the students laughed at the friendly disagreement. Sanchez, taking better notice of the float, saw artistic presentations of humanists through history and these complemented the projections from the screens. In addition, flowers and plants decorated the space between the monitors.

"She doesn't always contradict me," Sinclair told Sanchez in a congenial manner.

Asma scowled and began to tap several icons on her tablet.

"I transferred more quotes," Asma explained to Sinclair. "Look."

A new set of quotes appeared that caught the attention of the Priority Club members who began to point to them.

One quote read: "Religion is regarded by the common people as true, by the wise as false, and by the rulers as useful."

"Gibbons," Asma said haughtily.

"Don't escalate things," Sinclair gave her a friendly warning. "We have believers in our club, too."

"Um," Asma moaned and replaced the abrasive quote on her tablet.

Sinclair felt nervous, and this added to Sanchez's uneasiness.

"Mr. Sanchez will lecture for us one day," Sinclair revealed, hoping to divert everyone's attention away from the rivalry of the two clubs.

"Mr. Sanchez?" one of the students questioned.

"Yes," Sinclair commanded. "He'll be the man . . . how many times do I have to tell you."

"Three thousand," an anonymous voice shouted from behind the float.

Sinclair laughed.

"Hello," a timid girl's voice welcomed Sanchez from the top of the float.

"Hey!" "Hello!" "Hi!" "All right!" An aggregate of voices instantly welcomed him.

"Hi," Sanchez waved to the timid girl and to the others.

"Come up and help," a friendly voice suggested to Sanchez.

"Give him a sec," Asma interrupted to cut off the invitation.

So they quickly returned to work and their self-absorbed conversations.

Asma, taking the initiative, approached Sanchez and placed the tablet in front of him.

"Check out what we have for the display," she encouraged. "What do you think?"

Sanchez leaned back to focus on the screen. Historical images and phrases continued to appear and dissolve with coordination and creativity. He looked down to see the same script and images play on the tablet as they did on the monitors.

"This is very professional," Sanchez commented.

"Thanks," Asma said tepidly, expecting more enthusiasm.

Next year she would have to break him in.

"Where's Mr. Sinclair?" Sanchez asked, trying to pull away.

Exasperated, Asma made a quick visual search. "He's probably under the float," Asma said contemptuously. "He has such a brilliant insight into history and teaching. What a waste! You know what he wants to do for rehabilitation?"

"I can guess," Sanchez said, letting her control the flow of the conversation.

"Engineering," she told him disgustingly.

An unknown voice booed. Some members laughed afterwards. Asma ignored them.

"Engineering," she repeated as if Sanchez didn't hear. "Isn't that bourgeois?"

"I suppose," Sanchez replied, scrutinizing her allusion. He tried not to contest her.

Asma, noticing Sanchez's skepticism, expounded on her thinking: "I mean, our society is too technological. Don't get me wrong. I like technology and innovations. I use them. But now we learn from computers at school, and the humanities have been divested. If you want to study. . . ah, philosophy, for example . . . well, they put you in front of a virtual program. The philosophy is sanitized and follows a politically correct agenda. Only facts are given and no opinions. There's no insight . . . no interpretation. Boring! A teacher . . . a real person is needed."

"But that's where you get bias," Sanchez disingenuously used the ivory-tower arguments.

"Bias?" Asma digested the counterargument. "You need bias. . . . That's the point. A teacher has to give you other people's biases, so you can have an informed idea. How can you know anything without information? You need alternatives!"

"But you can get that . . . those biases from virtual lectures," Sanchez gently continued his argument. "You can go out and do the research."

Frustrated and flummoxed, Asma stared at him. Silently, every club member paused to eavesdrop on the discussion. "Wow!" Asma exclaimed. "You're like my dad." Her evaluation suddenly caused Sinclair to reappear from under the float.

"Tell me how," Sanchez probed, feeling elated with the exchange.

"Not like my dad exactly," she corrected herself and noticed that the other members were listening. She then made eye contact with Sinclair. "Mr. Sinclair," she pleaded. "Mr. Sanchez doesn't get it. They've brainwashed him."

Sanchez almost guffawed.

"What's your opinion?" Sinclair invited her to continue.

"He doesn't know what kids are like today," Asma spoke with exasperation. "It's like the whole system is screwed up from the top down!" She looked up at the members for support. "The students are lazy," Asma declared bluntly. "They just want to learn what they have to learn and spit it out for a good grade. Mr. Sanchez, no one is going to make the effort to look it up for altruistic reasons. Some may. But kids will cheat and find a shortcut. That's the way it is."

Sanchez saw that the club members were waiting for his response, and Sinclair gave him a slight nod of approval to continue. "You're right," Sanchez admitted. "I was the same. All my friends were the same. We cheated and looked for shortcuts. But there was one big difference from what I noticed after a couple of months here." He waited a moment.

"Yeah?" Asma waited impatiently.

"I had good teachers who caught me in the act," Sanchez revealed. "They made me look at myself and my motivations. It works on some and on others it won't."

"See," Asma spoke triumphantly. She unconsciously held up her tablet like a trophy winner. "I told you we need good teachers. . . . They don't get it."

"They?" Sanchez sought to clarify. "The administration . . . the system?"

"Who else?" she answered scathingly. "I hope you stay now. I still want Mr. Sinclair here."

"Me, too," Sanchez conceded and offered her a friendly smile.

Asma, delighted, smiled back and began to turn her attention to her tablet and the float.

"I'm going to take Mr. Sanchez with me," Sinclair excused himself and his colleague.

They walked past the Priority Club's float and saw Stile lurking about and fraternizing with its members. They ignored each other. Making a wide path around the float, Sinclair waited until they were a safe distance away.

"You scored, kid," Sinclair said in a congratulatory tone.

"What?" Sanchez asked, confused.

"Don't you get it?" Sinclair demanded to know. "They love you. Well, . . . Asma does. If she does, then she'll tell them to worship you."

"I don't want to be worshipped," he replied and continued to walk towards his car in the parking lot.

"Hey," Sinclair yelled, skipping a bit to catch up. "She is a fire-cracker."

Sanchez stopped and faced Sinclair. "Did you send the guest lecturer forms to the college?" he demanded.

"Yes," Sinclair spoke truthfully. "They probably will wait until you pass your observation review the first semester."

"They told me the same thing," Sanchez confirmed with disappointment.

"Voilà!" Sinclair declared, humorously holding up his arms. "That's all the French I know . . . except for some choice words. You know?"

"We all learn the choice words first," Sanchez said humorously. Then, turning serious, he confessed, "Now . . . I know why you like teaching. It's thrilling to share an idea . . . to make a connection . . . to be in a conversational debate with a young person. They're so open and absorbing . . . and we're killing them with empty, cold facts. But I don't know if I am right for the job. She's right . . ."

"Right?" Sinclair questioned.

"It's bourgeois," Sanchez said, quoting Asma.

Sinclair nodded agreeably at the allusion. The cliché was apropos.

"You're going to be bourgeois, too," Sanchez warned him. "Engineering?"

"I have my books and ideas still," he explained. "All those years of teaching will stay with me."

"But your mind . . . and your soul will wither," Sanchez warned him

"Maybe," Sinclair conceded. "The options are thin for me. The law states I can't remain in teaching."

Sanchez had a question but decided to wait for a better time. "I got to go," he said, excusing himself as he walked to his car. "Tomorrow my university supervisor is coming."

"You'll do great," Sinclair encouraged him.

"Really?" Sanchez disagreed. "I'm failing Adolescent Health. And you know why?"

"No." Sinclair tried to guess. "You didn't study?"

"Ah," Sanchez burst out laughing.

Sinclair waited for him to stop. "Go ahead," Sinclair pushed, suppressing a giggle.

"Do you know which way your erection leans?" Sanchez tried to maintain a serious tone.

Sinclair was shocked. "I have no idea what you asked," he admitted. "That was on the test? Shit! Is there a direction?"

"Well," Sanchez consoled him. "I feel better for failing. You don't know either."

They both laughed at the joke together.

"Tomorrow's observer shouldn't ask you the same question tomorrow," Sinclair assured him. "It would be . . . inappropriate." They laughed again.

"Thanks. See you."

They shook hands and Sinclair watched Sanchez enter his car and race out of the parking lot. When the car drove away, he discretely looked down at his crotch. "Maybe," he guessed, "to the left? Um?"

Chapter 9

November 2023
Sinclair

Friday afternoon: before the annual high school homecoming, chaos ensued, as deranged adolescent outbursts disrupted life on campus. Administrators and teachers gave up teaching and released their students to the explosive entertainments in the gym. They called it a pep rally. Sanchez escorted his fanatical students to the gym. On the way, an amorphous gathering of wandering students transformed into a horde of rowdy teenagers, aching to push their way into the gym.

The sudden influx of students created a jam outside the gym doors. Security and administrators rushed forward in an attempt to maintain some order. Fortunately, the students regrouped with a limited amount of self-control, but the sheer numbers of hormone-crazed humans caused the laws of the chaos theory to take hold.

Stile, who was wearing plaid oversized trousers with suspenders, stood close to the pulsating mob with a bullhorn and shouted threats and pleas with both vitriolic and kindly interspersions.

"Hey," he shouted. "Slow down, please. You guys . . . you guys . . . don't push. If I see anyone pushing, . . . they get detention . . . in-house suspension. I mean it! Hey, . . . please, . . . come on, guys. Get along now."

The bullhorn bawled repeatedly.

Slowly, two fragments of the mob caught Sanchez in a vise-like grip and involuntarily pushed him towards the gym's doors. Several new classes had arrived and added to the pressure at the doors. Frozen, Sanchez incredulously watched himself pushed uncontrollably forward until a familiar voice broke his rising panic.

"Sanchez!" Sinclair shouted at the top of his lungs. "Come here!" Sanchez forced his body to turn around, and he saw his mentor and several other teachers a few yards away, standing on the stone lunch benches in the quad.

"Come up here!" Sinclair screamed and waved him over.

Sanchez gave a hard push and broke away from the pulsating crowd. Stile caught sight of him before a sudden lurch of students distracted him and again redirected his energies.

"Stop," Stile warned them. "Step back and wait your turn. You . . . you . . . back off!"

Sanchez joined Sinclair and climbed to the top of the bench. "I always wait here," Sinclair smugly told him. "Too old to be pushed around."

Sanchez watched the mob begin to shrink as they squeezed through the doors like dried toothpaste. "Yeah," he agreed wholeheartedly.

"We'll go through when the crowd gets smaller," Sinclair added. Like rubbernecking eyewitnesses at the sight of a traffic accident, they observed—after a long ten minutes—that the horde was dwindling.

"So," Sinclair spoke normally when the crowds diminished. "What gives this morning?"

"What?" Sanchez asked, being caught off guard.

"The professor?" Sinclair jostled his memory. "How did the observation go?"

"Oh." Sanchez remembered the meeting. "Fine."

"Just fine?" Sinclair questioned.

Sanchez looked around to see if anyone were listening, but the other teachers, who had been standing on the benches, began to descend and stroll towards the gym doors.

"Yeah? OK," Sanchez assured him. "He told me about my lecture . . . the requirements. . . . The paperwork has gone through, and I have to wait for the official approval next semester."

Sinclair cautiously climbed down, too, and Sanchez joined him. Unlike the others, they remained behind, continuing to converse near the lunch benches.

"He was very congenial," Sanchez explained slowly. "We talked about what I do, and he was sympathetic about my not being able to lecture right now. He admitted that it would be hard to lecture as a first-year teacher. Basically, there was nothing for him to really see or talk about. I did mention you."

"Really?" Sinclair asked curiously.

"He said you were one of the best," Sanchez said. "And, if I get a chance to lecture with you, it would be a big personal and professional plus."

"Thanks," Sinclair responded. He waited a moment and raised an eyebrow as he looked at Sanchez. "But that's not all?"

"No," Sanchez admitted uneasily. "He told me he knows my husband."

"Very interesting," Sinclair answered with a mocking German accent.

"What?" Sanchez asked, confused.

"Go on," Sinclair encouraged him. Their time was running out since most of the students had entered the gym, and the administrators had begun to eye them. Stile joined the remaining group of students and entered the gym. Immediately, from inside the building, his bullhorn blasted orders and threats.

"He told me that my partner wanted me to pursue the law," Sanchez confessed. "I told him I like teaching. But . . ."

"But?" Sinclair encouraged him to continue.

"I don't know since I don't have enough hands-on experience," he relayed awkwardly. "Debating a student like Asma is not professional evidence of my qualifications."

"It is for most teachers," Sinclair joked.

Sanchez laughed and agreeably nodded. "I need more time," he said. "Really more time with the kids. You understand?"

"I do," Sinclair answered skeptically because for some reason, Sanchez's words did not ring completely true.

"What's the rest of it?" he probed.

The question surprised Sanchez.

"It's that obvious?" Sanchez asked and smiled.

"We're out of time," Sinclair pointed out. Everyone had entered the building, and the doors were closed. "We can talk later or right now?"

"OK," Sanchez noticed they were alone. "I've got a feeling that my partner is working behind the scenes to get me into law school."

"An offer you can't refuse?" Sinclair concluded. "So you can't let a good thing go?"

"Not without knowing more about this job," Sanchez clarified. "You can only say no once. You know how it goes."

"Right." Sinclair understood and sighed. "The politics of refusing a career," he informed Sanchez, "means you would close the door to any future opportunities until you reach rehabilitation in forty years."

"You," Sanchez noted, "sound like you have personal experience?"

"I do," he admitted boldly. "It's the text of my life at this time."

"Got you," Sanchez said, remembering his rehabilitation status. "I'm too self-absorbed."

"Naturally," he conceded. "We all are."

Running through the quad, Pierce appeared and dashed towards the gym, but not before he gave Sanchez and Sinclair a cautionary glare. He opened the doors, and a tsunami of air horns and music exploded into the quad, and Pierce's forward movement was fleetingly hampered. When the doors closed, serenity returned, except for the echoes of the muffled din.

"We've got to go," Sanchez told him and began to walk to the entrance.

"But that's not the problem," Sinclair called out. "Is it?"

Sanchez stopped and turned around.

"There's something else?" he pushed the subject.

"Later," Sanchez turned back. "I got to go sit with my kids."

"They're waiting. Don't worry," Sinclair sarcastically assured him. "Wait!"

Sanchez ignored him. Sinclair watched him open the doors and enter the hullabaloo. He accompanied the recalcitrant students who began to climb the long bleachers and sit on the right side of the gym.

Sinclair leisurely followed his protégé into the gym. There, a colleague—a mature Hispanic woman—stood near the door, where she positioned herself away from the clamoring students climbing up the bleachers. Seeing him, she immediately touched his hand.

"We never talk," she spoke reproachfully to Sinclair. "Are you avoiding me?"

Her voice surprised Sanchez, who recognized her. "Hey," he said. "Laura?"

She leaned over and kissed Sanchez on the cheek. "Hay is for horses," she reprimanded him. "How are you?"

Sinclair looked at the bleachers and then at her. Laura, also a rehabilitation candidate, was observing him sympathetically. They had been colleagues and friends for over thirty years and had often shared their confidential thoughts and experiences. Recently, she had lost her husband to cancer. In many ways, Sinclair loved her like a sister.

"I see you have a student teacher?" she inquired.

"He's doing fine," Sinclair assured her. "He just has some growing to do."

"Like us?" she poked his conscience.

Sinclair felt like an incorrigible boy waiting in the principal's office. "Sure," he meekly answered her and smiled sadly. They stopped talking when the activities began. Sanchez had disappeared. Sinclair looked for him among the bleachers, but he could not find him.

Stile stood in the middle of the gym floor and handed his bullhorn to a student aide who, in turn, handed him a wireless microphone. "Everybody sit down," Stile implored. "We have to start right away."

Suddenly the lights dimmed, and there was an uproar of shouts, whistles, catcalls, and hoots.

"OK," Stile announced loudly. "Here's our first guest . . . Mr. Ugly."

Abruptly, the students erupted with enthusiastic cheers, and the bleachers shook from the pressure of their uncontrollable anticipation. Immediately, Stile dashed to his left and hid among the administrators and teachers who stood at the side of the gym.

"Here it comes," Laura laughed. "Today will be good."

"Better than normal?" Sinclair was doubtful. He was still looking for Sanchez and wondered if he was watching the activities.

"Look!" she encouraged him to pay attention.

A young woman, wearing a man's toupee and a handlebar mustache, skipped onto the gym floor with a headphone and mouthpiece. She wore hobo clothes and extra large Oxford shoes.

"Let me introduce you to our contestants," she shouted. "Miss Uglies!"

From the far end of the gym, five young men dressed in drag escaped through the shadows of the lower bleachers and pranced onto the floor as they gyrated their bodies in provocative ways. They wore outlandish clothes, and their fake breasts projected far beyond what was naturally normal for mammalian glands. Following the contest rules, they had made every effort to be ugly. Hairy legs burst out of seamless stockings, and five-o'clock shadows blended unnaturally with their red face blush and excessive eye makeup.

"Our first contestant," the emcee announced.

A boy, wearing a purple bikini and spike heels, stepped forward. In fact, they all were scantily clad. "I'm Miss Bruta," he introduced himself, sticking his tongue out like Mick Jagger and prancing about the floor.

Another introduced himself as "Miss Fea." He then threw the audience a dramatic wet kiss and shook his ass in their direction.

"Is this art?" Sinclair questioned in embarrassment over the students' display. No one heard him. Instead howls and cheers shook the gym.

Many male students whistled, inviting the boys on a date. "I can see your cock!" a student jeered, followed by catcalls and more whistles.

"You have this happen in our day?" Laura shouted in Sinclair's ear.

Sinclair shook his head and watched with an open mouth. Escalating their behavior, the crowd became more rowdy, and their shouts became more obscene. Nervously, the administrators began to fan out, and Stile shouted into his microphone.

"All right," he screamed. "Hey!"

No one listened. He spoke into the emcee's ear.

"Be sure you vote on Monday," the emcee implored and waved to everyone as she strutted off the gym floor.

Using the microphone like a baton, Stile waved the Miss Ugly contestants off the gym floor.

They toed the line and followed the emcee off the gym floor, while they seductively displayed their curvatures and artificial enhancements to the audience. When they departed, the noise diminished to an annoying rumble. Seeing the atmosphere improving, the faculty members and administrators moved away from the walls and towards the front of the gym.

"Wow!" Sinclair exclaimed. "I couldn't think."

"It's not my ears," Laura disagreed. "It's my eyes!"

"You'll never recover," Sinclair joked. "You should see . . ."

His next words were cut off as Stile introduced the sport teams.

"Here come the football players!" he shouted so hard into his microphone, that there was a screeching back-feed.

The football coach replaced Stile and introduced the players, beginning with the captain of the team. Laura moved closer to Sinclair when the nearby faculty joined a congregation of school government leaders. The football players marched out to cheers and congratulatory roars.

"I played football for a while in high school," Sinclair proudly told Laura, "until I dislocated my wrist."

"Youth," Laura commented, "how fast it passes."

"Don't worry," Sinclair corrected her, "they're promising we can get it back."

"Crap," she dismissed the proposition.

"Sure," he continued, "the poetry of life is only given once."

"Poetry?" Laura questioned.

Sinclair looked directly at her, and before turning his attention to the team, he explained what he meant. "It's the innocent belief that it's all in front of you. There is so much to love and be excited about at this age. So much to discover. Life is filed with promises."

"You a cynic?" Laura felt uncomfortable about his musings.

"No," he dismissed the notion. "If I were, I wouldn't believe that today's kids could still enjoy that poetry. Medical science can't take it away from their DNA. The system is trying."

Laura reflected on his words and remained silent.

"We become so tired at this point," he added sadly. "They give us an extension. But physical energy doesn't supplement the enthusiasm. I can't imagine enjoying another eighty years of work. I know the score. Life for work. If not, you can look behind the other door and die."

"With dignity," Laura injected ironically, "not me."

"Dignity?" he repeated. "Death is death. All my cells and molecules have been fighting to escape this visceral prison. I'm just delaying the inevitable."

"You're really cheering us up," Laura commented scornfully. "Maybe you need to take a sabbatical?"

"A what?" Sinclair asked, confused. .

The option of a life sabbatical was not familiar to him.

"You didn't know?" Laura questioned.

An escalation of cheers, when the coach welcomed the cheerleaders, interrupted their conversation. The girls, with LED pom-poms, rushed to the center stage and began some low-gravity stunts. Commencing with a dance, they waved their pom-poms that glowed in synchronized, flashing colors. Then breaking into three groups of five, they formed a pyramid. One of the cheerleaders—the smallest of the group—climbed to the top of the human pyramid, and she was hurled into the air. Two other small cheerleaders followed her. Ascending for a moment and seeming to hang in midair, they exchanged positions and formed new groups. The pom-poms flashed in the school's colors as the cheerleaders' uniforms electronically matched the hues. They repeated the exercise three times and received a raucous standing ovation.

"Incredible," Sinclair declared, sharing the students' jubilation.

"I remember doing that," Laura leaned over and told him.

He looked at her in disbelief, and she waved her finger.

"We didn't have *neg-grav* shoes," she admitted. "But I had a great body."

"You did," he said, raising his eyebrow in emphasis as he remembered when he first saw her thirty years ago.

So," Laura asked, "ready to go?"

"What?" Sinclair asked.

The soccer team arrived, and there was another eruption of applause and cheers. Laura tugged Sinclair's elbow and then turned around. Sinclair watched her walk rapidly towards the doors, and she shot him a glance before stepping out. He cautiously followed her outside where she waited for him on a lunch bench. When he opened the doors, the rush of the escaping noise pushed against his back like the wind on a sail.

"Thanks for coming," she said. "I want to try those special shoes."

Sinclair smiled agreeably, sensing a ringing in his ears.

"You're going to tell me about the sabbatical?" he encouraged her to continue.

She nodded and affectionately touched his forearm.

"Look," she began uneasily. "You can take a break and not jump into the new job."

"Why didn't I hear about that?" Sinclair queried. "It's sort of hard to hide that kind of info."

"Yes," Laura acknowledged and looked towards the gym doors. "But they do want to hide it. If you ask any counselor or rehabilitation attorney, she will tell you."

"Ah," Sinclair said, not wishing to interrupt Laura's revelation. "But there is a catch?"

"Sure," Laura spoke frankly and gently slapped his shoulder. "Always, my friend. The price is delay . . . an imposed acceptance . . . or death."

"Really?" Sinclair whistled knowingly. "I get it. . . . They can stick me in limbo."

"Just to punish you," Laura clarified. "Or . . . if you're a real pain in the ass, give you another assignment."

"An offer you can't refuse," Sinclair concluded pessimistically. "And if you're a real pain . . ."

"No more life-extending dope," Laura finished his thoughts. "You retire and die before your time."

"Well," Sinclair rejected the idea, "I won't really die before my time."

A flash of anger crossed her face. "It's before my time," she declared emphatically. "I lost my youthful poetry long ago. I'm alone now. Maybe life is boring, but I don't want to die young. Life is great because it's life. I want to live. You get one chance only."

"You do," Sinclair confirmed philosophically. "But it's quality for me, not quantity. We got too much quantity, Laura. That's the problem."

"I bet you won't feel that way when you're on the gurney, and they shoot the poison into your veins," she mocked his stoicism.

"No," Sinclair admitted. "I'll be a coward, but the same thing will happen later . . . in eighty years or a hundred. Then . . . what do you do?"

"I can wait," Laura stood up defiantly.

Sinclair remained seated, hoping to coax her to sit down again.

"Why tell me?" he asked curiously. "Why recommend to me something you automatically reject as toxic?"

Unexpected, the school bell rang.

"I..." Laura tried to answer, but the gym doors burst open, and students rushed out.

They instinctively walked ahead of the crowd towards the administration building fifty yards away.

"Mr. Sinclair," a familiar voice called out. Sinclair stopped to see Asma and hundreds of students approaching him. When he turned around again, Laura had vanished into the crowd.

"You looking for someone?" Asma asked. He took one more searching glance, but he could not find her.

"No," Sinclair lied. "It doesn't matter. What's up?"

"We need you to sign the entry form," she said anxiously. "We need it, or Mr. Stile won't let us show our float."

"OK," Sinclair accepted her reasoning and followed her to the office.

When he reached the office, he looked back towards the gym for Laura, and instead, he saw Sanchez standing alone. He waved to him.

November Intermission

Smith arrived at the homecoming events with trepidation. He caught a glimpse of his unrequited love, Helen, but she was working near the concession stand. After the game, he promised himself to offer her a ride home. The thought cheered him up. Using a mechanical handgrip, he picked up discarded litter and dropped it into a black bag. By the event's conclusion late in the evening, he had removed large piles of discarded trash that included torn banners, flyers, food, and drink cans. Luckily, Rubio and Stile had recruited club volunteers to assist the janitors.

As expected, Rubio had assigned Smith the location under the bleachers where inconsiderate spectators dropped trash onto dying patches of grass and soil below. Dragging a small specially designed container, he ducked under the bleachers' cross support beams and used his handgrip to lift and dispose of the litter, as he cursed all the while. He collected an abundance of pocket coins and change, including some bills. Those he kept. However, every fortuitous gain invited a miserable loss.

"Shit," Smith exclaimed, removing a soiled condom from a food wrapper. "How do they fuck in this place? Animals! Yuck!" he angrily spoke to himself. The discovery of a soiled condom did not disturb him as much as its presence reminded him that he had been chaste for too long. He began to pine for his coworker, Helen, who coyly played with his feelings.

When he finished one section of the bleachers, Smith abruptly pulled himself out from under the grating, accidently striking his head against a sharp aluminum support beam. The unfortunate accident caused the bleachers to vibrate slightly. Instinctively, he dropped his handgrip and threw it to the ground.

"Aw!" he screamed. "Fucker!"

Some nearby club members stopped to watch the old janitor limp away as he pressed a handkerchief to his head. Stile saw him and detected blood soaking the cloth. He ran to tell Rubio.

"Ah," Smith moaned furiously. "Shit. Goddamn!"

Smith pulled the handkerchief away to look at it. Clogged clumps of congealing blood clung to the fabric. Immediately, a trickle of blood flowed onto his temples and dripped into his eyes. Annoyed, he wiped his eyes, and in the process spread his blood to the back of his hands and uniform.

"Smith!" Rubio yelled from nearby.

From the football field, Rubio, carrying his protruding stomach like a wheelbarrow during a country fair race, darted frantically towards Smith. Several club members reached Smith first.

"Hey," one of the club members called for help, as Rubio and Stile came up.

"Stand back," Stile barked, as if he were using a bullhorn.

Examining the wound, Stile saw a gaping split in Smith's scalp that quickly welled with blood. He thought he caught a glimpse of the gray matter beneath the fractured skull. Soon, more people arrived to assist Smith. "Gross," one student commented in disgust.

Rubio, snarling, offered Smith a towel. He took a quick look at the head wound and tried to try to stanch the bleeding.

"Get that shit away from me," Smith said, swiping at the cloth. "That shit's dirty. You'll give me an infection."

He growled at Rubio who backed off like a scared lion trainer. Stile gave him another cloth, and Smith gently took it and carefully placed it on his head.

"Let's go," Stile suggested. "You need medical attention."

"Take him straight to emergency," Rubio recommended.

Stile and several students helped to escort Smith to Stile's car, safely avoiding any contact with his blood. Smith painfully shuffled along several yards before angrily turning around.

"This is worker's comp!" he reminded Rubio.

Rubio stared back in confusion. Gently, Stile guided Smith back towards the parking lot. "You have to get to the doctor," he reminded him.

Smith shrugged and trudged to the parking lot. When he reached the car, a small entourage of curious students was waiting, gawking at the strange little old man.

"Be careful," Stile kindly told Smith as he got into the car. He threw the soaked cloth on the grass and accepted a donation from a student to catch the blood before it began to trickle down Smith's scalp.

Smith sat miserably in his seat; he was secretly pleased that the wound would give him some time away from his job and Rubio. The pleasure, like all minor triumphs, evaporated quickly. When he looked out the car window, he saw Helen speaking to Rubio who would probably drive her home.

"Shit," he groaned in a lament as Stile started the fuel-cell-powered sedan and drove off to the nearest hospital.

Sinclair sat home alone on a Saturday after spending Thanksgiving with his children. His wife, Rachel, had talked to the whole family on the home monitor, but she and Sinclair did not exchange too much personal information, except financial concerns. She had promised to try to visit during winter break, but Sinclair knew that she would not make the journey. Her promise only placated the family, and everyone understood her fabrication as a good intention.

Rachel would stay in Japan. Therefore, resigning himself to the fact that he would be alone a while longer, Sinclair worked on his motorbike with more gusto in his open garage. His new spark plug had arrived; it took a minute to figure out, and then he took the gamble to install it. Siphoning some gasoline out of a sports drink bottle, he started the engine. After a few hard pedal kicks, the engine ignited and vibrated violently for several minutes. Surprisingly, it sputtered, coughed, and died. He tried again, and it would not start. After several unsuccessful attempts, he realized the obvious—there was not enough gasoline in the sports drink bottle.

"Yo!" a familiar voice shouted from outside.

Turning around, he saw the mail carrier holding a letter. He was an independent carrier in his fifties. He dressed in civilian clothes and used his own car as a subcontractor for the U.S. Postal Service. Mail carriers rarely made personal deliveries unless they were imperative.

"You have to sign," he explained abruptly. "Government business."

Sinclair switched off the battery and put down the makeshift gas tank. He then instinctively felt for a pen in his sweatpants until the mail carrier stuck a small tablet in front of his face.

"Here," he directed Sinclair to sign. Annoyed at the interruption, Sinclair smirked and signed the tablet with the attached stylus. "OK," the carrier said and handed him the letter. Then he unceremoniously marched off to his truck.

Sinclair ignored the carrier as he gaped at the return address on the letter. It was from the Rehabilitation Department for Retired Americans.

"Great," he bemoaned the probable contents of the letter. Apprehensively, he tore open the letter and scanned the contents. He carefully read it several times. After passing over the preface and introductory pleasantries, Sinclair focused on one specific section of the letter:

You are tentatively approved for a one-year sabbatical beginning at 12:00 A.M. Eastern Time on the official first day of retirement. The date is to be determined with this office. Official notice will be sent when you have completed the required documentations and stipulations . . .

His smart watch suddenly vibrated, and he checked his e-mail. A copy of the letter had been texted. "Redundant bureaucracy," Sinclair mumbled aloud.

He wondered if he had made the right decision. Sinclair quickly decided he did since he had nothing to lose although Laura thought otherwise. A question still lingered in his mind as to why she shared information she personally disdained and rejected. Unlike his colleague, he was not sure about his future. He needed more time to decide. Another vibration on his smart watch reminded him that he had a meeting with his counselor.

"I love Thanksgiving," he commented and gratefully refilled his empty sports drink bottle, returning to his inoperable motorbike.

Chapter 10

December 2023
Sanchez

"Ah . . . three . . . what?"
—Fernando Smith (The Janitor)

Sanchez sat with his computer tablet on his favorite lounge chair made from natural plant fibers that imitated leather. Time was running out, and he had forgotten to buy a Christmas gift for his mentor. His partner, Nick, stood behind Sanchez and watched him scan through an array of images of Christmas gift suggestions. He keyboarded Sinclair's profession into the search engine. The website lamentably revealed common items such as books, electronic devices, gift cards, and passes.

"Shit," Sanchez cursed.

"Stuck?' Nick, curious, asked.

He removed his smartphone and placed it on the coffee table next to Sanchez.

Sanchez stopped his search, and he looked up.

"Where in the hell did you come from?" he asked, annoyed by the interruption. .

Sanchez utterly disliked surprise visits, especially surprise birthday parties.

"Sorry," Nick apologized and walked around Sanchez to sit across from his partner.

"I can't find anything," Sanchez spoke in frustration. He shook the tablet and returned to his search. "This stuff seems OK, but it's not what I want to give him."

"Ah." Nick thought it over. "Did you narrow your search to a couple of other categories?"

"No," Sanchez admitted bluntly. "I can't think."

Nick watched Sanchez struggle with the tablet for a minute.

"Are you in love?" Nick joked.

Shocked, Sanchez glared at him. "What the fuck!" he exclaimed angrily. "You've got to be shitting me!"

Nick smiled and raised his hand in a gesture of peace.

"Joking," he confided. "Really!" He crossed his heart and held up his fingers in a Boy Scout salute.

"I'm not in the mood," Sanchez warned him. "The Christmas party is next week. I got his name in the Secret Santa gift exchange.

"Wow!" Nick spoke mockingly and waved his hand. "I bet it just happened like that!"

Sanchez studied Nick and ignored his sarcasm.

"Whatever or whoever," Sanchez returned to his search. "I got to find a gift. I know Stile fixed the Santa part."

"Yeah," Nick said with scorn. "No kidding."

Sanchez struggled with his search until Nick interrupted him. "Hey," he called out, "wait!"

Sanchez stopped again and looked up impatiently. "No more jokes," he pleaded. "Please."

"No," Nick responded honestly. "Listen. "Doesn't he like to do something . . . with . . . bicycles? You told me about it."

"Shit," Sanchez felt a surge of relief erase his anxiety. "I forgot. He's building a motorbike."

Nick stood up, walked delightedly over to Sanchez's chair and observed him scan through pages of motorbike accessories.

"They got tons of stuff," Sanchez confirmed happily. "Great. Thanks. You're the best."

Sanchez smiled at Nick and continued to scan. Nick then bent down and kissed him on the forehead. He returned to his chair and waited for Sanchez to finish his search. After a while, he stopped waiting and interrupted his partner. "Did you find anything?" he inquired with curiosity as he stood in front of Sanchez.

"No," Sanchez spoke with frustration. "First, there's nothing, and now there's too much!" He continued to scrutinize the items online until Nick's impatient posture interrupted his concentration. "Go ahead," Sanchez invited him to speak, knowing Nick had something to contribute. Sanchez made the supreme effort to control himself, as Nick sat down, nervously smiling.

"Look," he began, "there's not a lot of time."

"I'm healthy," Sanchez quipped and laughed. "I won't die soon."

"This is serious," Nick dismissed his witticism. "You've got to decide."

"I know," Sanchez conceded. "But I told you . . . I have to try one lecture at least. It's special to me."

Nick inhaled deeply. "Sure," he pressed his partner. "But then it might be too late. Lecturing students is outdated. Passé! They flip classes now. It's all about collaborative learning and virtual school."

Sanchez spun over his tablet and slammed it on the chair's arm. "What's too late?' Sanchez argued. "I have a job. Nick , . . . I engaged in a discussion with a young girl I met during a homecoming event. To exchange ideas with her and to listen to her felt great. I really enjoyed seeing her express her thoughts and feelings. It made me feel good to know that I can have a positive effect on these kids."

Nick felt his blood pressure rise, but he measured his explanation. "Sentimentality! That's all. It's not too late for teaching." Then he reminded Sanchez, "It might be too late for law school. Careers aren't so flexible if you've read the news lately."

Sanchez looked away and down at his tablet.

"I have a contact that can help you get into law school," Nick emphasized the opportunity. "We don't want to lose it."

"We?" Sanchez reminded him who needed to make the decision. "Is this person the anonymous entity who keeps sending you messages?" Sanchez pointed to the smartphone on the coffee table.

Nick ignored his question. "I don't get it," Nick responded irksomely and stood up. "Don't you want to do this together?"

Sanchez watched him quietly for a moment, and then he spoke with an even tone. "We are together," Sanchez pointed out, "aren't we?"

Nick shook his head and sat down again. "Don't be obtuse," Nick disagreed. "If not now, you will have to wait until rehabilitation."

"Maybe," Sanchez answered and prepared to challenge him. "I have a question?"

Nick gave him a querulous expression.

"Who's this contact?" Sanchez pressed on. He had been asking Nick this question for weeks with no satisfactory answer.

"I can't," Nick denied his request. "It's really confidential. I can't risk his position and career. But why can't you trust me?"

Sanchez stood up and faced down Nick.

"Why can't you trust me?" Sanchez countered him. "I thought we loved each other and were getting married. I don't know, Nick."

"You want to break up?" Nick demanded to know and stood up.

Sanchez waited and then affectionately touched Nick's hand as he explained his reasoning. "We're having some serious differences," Sanchez clarified. "You don't want me to look at this career path, and you can't trust me to keep a confidence. There's some mistrust going on here. Don't you see?"

Nick suddenly got red and pulled away.

"You are really goin' to blow it!" he warned Sanchez. "I just want a good career for you and a shot for us at making some money together. Don't you know that teachers have their salary supplemented by the government? You'll live at the poverty level."

"It's just money?" Sanchez tried to understand. "Money is important, but I need something more now. . . I think. Aren't we living together? Why can't we have our own careers?"

"But we have our plans, our dreams," Nick reminded him. "Things just don't change like this."

"I know," Sanchez admitted, trying to reach out to Nick, who stepped back a bit. "But things do change, and I feel I have to check this avenue out for myself. I'd hoped you would understand."

Nick remained quiet and looked down at his feet as he spoke. "If you take this course," Nick said sadly. "I can't promise to be here waiting in the end."

"Then you better make your decision, too," Sanchez warned him. Nick raised a teary eye and walked out of their home.

Sanchez sat alone, replaying the conversation they had just had. He began to tremble. The options were few, and his thoughts were interrupted when Nick's smartphone vibrated. Taking up the phone from the coffee table, he saw an encrypted message from Nick's secret contact.

"What did you get yourself into, Nick?" Sanchez wondered. "And what in the hell did I get myself in to?"

He put down the phone on the table. Reluctantly, he returned to his tablet and made a futile effort to find Sinclair a Christmas gift. His heart, unfortunately, was not into the search anymore.

The smartphone again began to vibrate.

Chapter 11

December 2023
Sinclair

Making reservations at a popular seafood restaurant had been Pierce's idea. He had decided to spend some money on the staff and hold the annual Christmas party off campus, away from prying parental eyes and gossiping students. During the evening, most of the staff trickled sporadically into the restaurant, hoping to be fashionably late. When Sinclair parked his car, he immediately noticed the school's club banners on display across the restaurant's façade. Each banner wished the public a happy holiday from Merry Christmas to Happy Kwanza and Happy Hanukah. Above the large building door, Asma had hung the red Free Speech Club banner above the large building's door and it overshadowed the other holiday banners.

"Greetings," Sinclair read aloud. "It's the Season of Reason."

Experiencing a conflict of annoyance and pride, he anxiously approached the restaurant's entrance, as he gripped tightly his Secret Santa gift for the exchange. Nervous perspiration from his hand had begun to soak into the gift-wrapping and ruin it. Adding to his anxiety, Stile arrived ahead of him and stood outside, also reading the Free Speech Club's declaration. A few incoherent murmurings dribbled from his mouth. From a close distance, Sinclair could not understand all the words, but the tone of his uncharitable comments was unambiguously clear.

"Mr. Sinclair!" he called out disapprovingly. "This is contrary to . . ." Flabbergasted, Stile left his thoughts hanging in midair.

"Nothing," Sinclair added with aplomb.

"What?" Stile demanded an explanation.

Sinclair felt the gift shift in his hand. The wrapping had torn away from the packaging. "Shit," he cursed, trying to peel the paper off his palm.

His effort was unsuccessful. Stile stared at Sinclair's predicament and almost forgot what he wished to say. He pointed in exasperation at the banner. "This can't be allowed!" he exclaimed.

Sinclair looked up at the Free Speech Club banner and then read the others. "Have you ever thought," Sinclair mused in a calm voice, "that others might be offended by these religious banners?"

"What?"" answered Stile, confounded by the suggestion. "You're making no sense!"

"It's a free country," Sinclair reminded him. "Think about it."

"What?" Stile repeated.

Sinclair ignored him and walked into the boisterous restaurant full of music and loud conversations. As he entered, Pierce stood beside a counselor who was speaking into his ear. Holding a drink, the director burst out laughing before making eye contact with Sinclair.

"Mr. Sinclair," Pierce shouted and waved to him over the loud conversations and blaring Christmas music.

Sinclair took a moment to adjust his eyes to the dim lighting, and then he walked awkwardly towards Pierce, as he wondered how he might fix the gift's tattered wrapping. Paper towels came to mind. The counselor made a quick comment and left Pierce. Sinclair saw the janitor, Smith, in one corner. He was conversing with the other janitors. They appeared to be the most spirited and rowdy of the group.

"Mr. Sinclair," Pierce repeated with a cheery smile. "Happy Season of Reason!""

"You too? Give me a break," Sinclair snapped. He quickly regretted it.

Pierce stared and promptly burst out laughing. "I bet you ran into Mr. Stile," he coyly suggested, offering Sinclair a conciliatory smile.

Sinclair accepted his olive branch and returned the smile with a handshake. "Sorry," he apologized. "Happy Kwanza, Hanukah, Christmas, and all of the above."

"Cheers," Pierce said and held up his drink. He looked thoughtfully at Sinclair and at his drink. "Sir," he uttered in a grave tone. "You need a holiday drink."

"You're right," Sinclair accepted the offer and searched for the bar.

He enjoyed being able to mix alcohol with his rehabilitation drugs.

"Back there," Pierce motioned with his drink. Wishing to avoid any official conversation, Pierce looked away.

"Mr. Pierce," a woman's voice could be heard above the hubbub.

Bleary-eyed, Pierce turned around. "Got my job to do," he spoke regretfully, and he parted with Sinclair with a wink.

Amanda, an oversized woman who taught English, rumbled dangerously towards Pierce. Wearing a cluster of Arizonan Native American silver and turquoise jewelry, she had applied too much makeup, and her clothes were disheveled. Her drink sloshed about, some spilling out as she approached. "Did I wish you Happy Holidays?" she greeted him and planted a wet kiss on his check. "We must all be jolly."

Pierce protected his drink and rotated away from her menacing grasp. She pivoted her body and snatched him. "Happy..." was all he spat out before he lost his breath in her bear hug.

Sinclair tried to sneak away. "Happy Holidays to you," Amanda wished Sinclair over Pierce's shoulder. "You pagan."

"Thanks," Sinclair accepted and raised his hand in cheer.

He used the interruption to slink away towards the bar, while trying to keep the gift's wrapping from completely tearing away. Fortunately, Amanda saved him from a confrontation with Stile, who angrily walked into the restaurant and began berating Pierce. Grabbing Sinclair, Amanda abruptly gave him her favorite bear hug and holiday kiss.

Sinclair, again, could only hear the tone of Stile's frustration as his words melted into the background noise of the crowd. He could almost feel some sympathy for Stile's predicament—almost.

"Mr. Sinclair!" a familiar voice screamed into his ear. Startled, Sinclair saw Vega, his counselor, wearing a Santa hat. His drink would be delayed.

"I'm Santa's helper," Vega said. He looked down at Sinclair's gift and then waved his finger from side to side. "You're on the naughty list," he announced gravely.

Sinclair looked down at his gift, too, and instinctively handed it to Vega. His eyes begged for help. "Well," Vega accepted the task. "I'll talk to Santa and put you on the nice list?" He produced a wide grin. "Happy Holidays," he wished Sinclair and gave him a spontaneous hug. Reluctantly, Sinclair returned the embrace.

"You must come and see me," he advised Sinclair. "The sabbatical must be carefully maneuvered."

"Right," Sinclair said. He wanted to avoid the topic. "Later? Can't we?"

Vega understood and respected his request. "I'll fix this," Vega promised, holding up the gift. "I know who it's for so I won't let you down."

Sinclair was curious to know how he would fix it, but he decided it was best to accept the offer at face value. "Thanks," Sinclair gratefully shook his hand.

Vega returned an affectionate smile and tucked the gift away under his arm. "I better hurry," he dismissed himself. "The exchange will happen soon. Go get something to eat."

Sinclair did not feel hungry as he watched Vega scuttle off into a thick gathering of drunken faculty members. "Nice to have one of Santa's elves on your side," he commented to himself, walking in the opposite direction.

As he continued wandering, he looked to share a few moments with Sanchez. Searching for him, Sinclair assumed Sanchez would find company among a small group of young teachers. Disappointingly, he could not find him.

Sanchez saw him first. "Hey," he called out.

Sinclair was startled to realize that his protégé had been standing only a few feet away.

"How long have you been there?" he asked with a smile, as an unfamiliar, jocular woman, holding a large, yellow drink, scurried by and awkwardly placed a Santa cap on Sinclair's head.

"Happy everything," she slurred and swallowed her drink. She gave him a quick peck on the check and disappeared back into the crowd.

"These people aren't all teachers, are they?" Sinclair questioned. He surveyed the restaurant and failed to recognize many partyers.

"First," Sanchez took the hat off Sinclair's head and placed it on his own. "I've always wanted one of these." Sinclair felt like objecting, but he grudgingly let the hat go.

"Definitely looks better on you," Sinclair said facetiously.

Sanchez tried to find a mirror to look at his hat. Instead, an opaque serving plate served the purpose. "You're right . . . looking good," he spoke proudly. "Thanks."

"Sure," Sinclair grunted. Sanchez was ecstatic, expressing genuine pleasure with his appearance. Seeing the hat naturally complement Sanchez's features, Sinclair happily accepted its loss.

"Oh," Sanchez said, trying to collect his thoughts while fingering the white felt above his brow. "I think most are teachers' guests, and some come off the streets."

"Wonderful," Sinclair remarked. He suddenly regretted coming. "I hate strangers."

"Yeah," Sanchez agreed, trying to fathom Sinclair's discomfort. "But after a few drinks everybody loves their neighbor."

"The golden rule," Sinclair mocked.

Sanchez chuckled and then motioned Sinclair towards the bar. "Are you hungry?" he asked.

"No," Sinclair replied, but he decided he wanted some artificial good cheer. "But I'll take a glass of red wine."

"OK," Sanchez agreed enthusiastically. "Let's toast to our first drink tonight." Sanchez asked the bartender for two glasses of red wine. As he handed the first glass to his mentor, he said, "Salute," in a toast, adding, "Cheers. To my first lecture next year!" With that, he downed his entire glass of wine.

"And to my last," Sinclair finished, taking a quick swallow of his drink. Sanchez stopped drinking but decided against saying anything. "Speaking of strangers," Sinclair added, and he took another long swallow of wine. "Where's your partner . . . uh . . . Nick?"

"Nick," Sanchez said, as he searched for a reasonable explanation for his absence, "Oh, he doesn't like these types of parties."

"You mean," Sinclair corrected him, "he doesn't like teachers." Sanchez opened his mouth to speak but remained silent, unconsciously staring into his drink. "Sorry," Sinclair sincerely apologized, feeling the need for some more wine.

"It's OK," Sanchez assured him, "we all have to deal with disappointments. We can't be on the same page with everything."

"No," Sinclair sadly agreed, thinking about his wife and their failing marriage. "We can't." Remorsefully, Sinclair could offer him no solace. Despite the music, conversations, shouts, and laughs surrounding them, they both felt isolated and alone in the large overexcited chamber.

"Attention," a loud voice boomed out. It was Vega. "It's time for the Santa exchange!" From the speakers, "Jingle Bells" played to the swishing sounds of a snowstorm accompanied by sleigh bells.

"Be careful where you stand," Vega mischievously warned everyone, "unless you want to be kissed under the mistletoe,"

A female squeal ripped across the clamor, and a math teacher jumped up to kiss an unidentified man standing under the mistletoe.

"Who's he?" Sanchez inquired in curiosity.

Sanchez strained to look but could not recognize the man who reciprocated with a more affectionate kiss. "One of those strangers," he concluded.

"She doesn't seem to mind," Sanchez sarcastically observed, and this caused Sinclair to burst out laughing.

As he finished the last of his drink, Sinclair turned to Sanchez and merrily ordered, "Get me another one."

Sanchez happily agreed and returned with two fresh glasses of the mediocre red wine. Raising his own, he flourished with, "Salute."

"¡Salud!" Sinclair repeated Sanchez's Spanish toast and took a long swallow, as his protégé did likewise.

"Cheers! Salute!" Vega shouted. "Happy Holidays, Mr. Sinclair." The crowd turned to look at Sinclair, and all the guests raised their drinks and yelled, "Cheers! Salute!" Applause followed. Sinclair maintained his composure, smiled, and, in return, raised his wine glass.

"Let's get to the gifts!" Vega refocused on the task at hand. "We all love gifts. . . . No?"

Laughter and roars of approval followed his call to action. He announced names and handed out gifts. Sinclair tried not to look at Sanchez and wondered whether Vega had fixed his wrapping. Slowly, the number of remaining gifts dwindled, and Sinclair began to feel nervous, thinking that Vega purposely had delayed his gift exchange. Sanchez also displayed some anxiety at the delay.

"Hey," Laura interrupted Sinclair's thoughts. She appeared dressed as an elf and was holding a tall, thin glass filled with a creamy white liquid. "You got the extension I hear?" she probed and offered him an affable smile.

Sinclair had not seen her for a while, and he still wanted to know her motivation. "Happy Holidays," he said, ignoring her question. "I'm waiting for the gifts."

"I see," she looked around and then at Vega. "I got a lawyer I can recommend to you."

"Thanks," Sinclair told her with cold frankness. "I got one, too."

"This lawyer you should contact," Laura clarified. "He told me that the extension wouldn't work for me. He might say the same to you. Or he can tell you if it will work for you. I just want you to do it safely."

"Why won't it work for you?" Sinclair demanded to know.

"Well, . . . that's the way it was for me," she spoke with reticence. Her cagey attitude began to erode his cheerful disposition further. "We'll talk after you see him," she counseled. "If not, . . . we'll forget about it." She gave him a kiss and cradled his arm warmly.

"Mr. Sinclair," Vega called out his name. Applause and whistles erupted spontaneously.

Laura released her grip and applauded heartily. Sinclair could not react, contemplating Laura's words. "Go," she whispered seductively in his ear.

He looked at her but could not read any deception in her expression. Sinclair saw only a pair of warm friendly eyes, belonging to a woman he had long loved as a friend and sister. Now, he wondered if he had misunderstood those feelings. Maybe they had once loved each other more deeply.

"Go," Sanchez insisted from behind, giving Sinclair a shove. He looked back at Sanchez who motioned for him to walk forward. Taking his cue, Sinclair felt slightly buoyant and walked cheerfully towards Vega, who reached out to give him his Santa exchange gift. Sinclair shook his hand, and more applause followed. He returned to Sanchez and discovered that Laura was gone.

"You see her?" Sinclair asked, anxiously looking around for Laura.

"She took off when you stepped away," Sanchez told him and eyed the gift Sinclair held. "It's from me. Open it."

"Oh," Sinclair uttered, suddenly aware of the Christmas gift. He tightly clutched it.

"Don't break it," Sanchez joked. Sinclair began gently to tear the wrapping without exposing the gift. "It won't break," Sanchez pressed him. "Really! Go ahead."

Sinclair looked at him and chortled, quickly tearing away at the wrapping. Several items fell out of his hands and flew to the floor. He picked them up with Sanchez's help. Examining the clear plastic bags, Sinclair recognized several motorcycle accessories: a pair of black gloves, a yellow mesh pullover shirt, and a pair of blue jeans.

"They're all tear-proof," Sanchez proudly pointed out, "and fire-resistant."

"Really?" Sinclair muttered, trying to forget about Laura. He realized that he had temporarily abandoned his motorbike project, and he made a private New Year's resolution to finish it early next year. "This is what I need to jump-start my project," he admitted cheerfully. "Wow! I can use these."

"I'm glad you like them," Sanchez responded, feeling a sense of relief.

Sinclair then reached out to him and gave him a quick hug. "Thanks again," he repeated. "Great."

"Mr. Sanchez," Vega called out. "Our new young educator; we all need more like him around here."

More applause was followed by hoots and cheers. Sanchez looked at Sinclair, who gave him a thumbs-up, and he hurried towards Vega. Pierce intercepted Sanchez and gave him a quick handshake. Awkwardly holding his own Christmas gifts tightly, Sinclair peered into the hazy darkness and watched Vega hand Sanchez his gift. He had repackaged it in a slightly larger box covered with reindeer, elves, and mistletoe wrapping. Sanchez returned to his place and held up the box.

"I can't wait," he keenly told Sinclair who continued to grip his loose gifts. He pulled at the corner tabs, and the box seemed to unfold automatically. A soft green tissue paper covered the gift box, and Sanchez looked curiously at Sinclair.

"Be careful with it," Sinclair advised him somberly. "Really!" Sanchez immediately expressed some distress. "It's not that fragile," Sinclair changed his tune.

Sanchez nodded and slowly removed the green paper. Underneath, a brown leather-bound book appeared. The edges were frayed a little.

"It's a rare classic from the eighteenth century," Sinclair explained. "A parallel text of Marcus Aurelius's *Meditations*. Latin and English. I thought you might like it."

"Like it?" Sanchez choked. "It's beautiful . . . too . . . valuable. I now have to learn Latin."

"Si vales, gaudeo. Ego valeo recte," Sinclair spoke. "If you're happy, I'm happy."Sanchez extended his hand to return the book, but Sinclair waved him off. "No," Sinclair spoke sternly. "You of all people will use it best."

"Where, . . . " Sanchez carefully opened the book and leafed through the first pages. "Where did you get this?"

"It's been in my collection," Sinclair said. "Now it's yours."

Sanchez read the Roman numerals on the title page. It dated the printing to 1789. He admired the woodcut figures of Greek gods. Caressing the page, he carefully closed the book and held it up like a monstrance. "I'll treasure it," he promised.

"No," Sinclair paternalistically told him. "Read it!"

Sanchez nodded and walked over to hug Sinclair.

"I love Santa gift exchanges," Vega shouted into the microphone and pointed to the two men. "Everyone have a good holiday. Ho, Ho, Ho!"

Sporadic laughs and applause followed as everyone returned to their cliques and their drinks.

"These will be needed," Sinclair said, returning to his accessories, "once I'm done with the bike."

"Can't ride without them," Sanchez advised.

"I won't," Sinclair promised. He took a casual examination of his surroundings and failed to see Laura in the crowd. Saddened, he returned his gaze to Sanchez who was gently and carefully placing the book back in its box. Sanchez held the box like a curator handling a priceless treasure.

"Happy . . . Happy," Vega repeatedly slurred and shouted into the microphone. "Jingle all the way!"

Joining the rowdy crowd, Sinclair cheered, raising his glass. His phone vibrated, startling him. He suspiciously looked at it and saw Laura's message. She had gone home. The message contained her attorney's contact information and an affectionate Christmas greeting. Sadly, he missed her and wondered if he just felt sorry for himself.

December Intermission

After the party, Smith arrived home to his small efficiency, which was a converted garage. Trembling, he held his smartphone and stared at Helen's contact name. After a few drinks and some careful maneuvering, she had spontaneously provided him with her number. Feeling a little sloshed, Smith gazed mindlessly at her number as a dark thought began to cross his mind. Maybe, he thought, the number was a fake. The thought terrified him despite the truth.

Slowly, still holding his phone, he eased himself into a comfortable chair and mentally reminisced, "Listen, baby," he recalled telling her. "You have not lived until you see an opera. It's beautiful."

A few hours ago at the party, she had beamed under the dim lights and Christmas decorations, as she ran the tip of her finger around the rim of her glass. Now back home, he returned to his memories. "I like music," she had told him as she coyly licked her lips.

Smith had fallen in love with her when she was first hired, and every janitor had already made a pass at her. They all failed. Smith never made any coarse remarks; he always showed her respect. Carefully he weighed his words, gestures, and actions. Helen's aloofness belied any jealousy on his part. Only Rubio, the man who hired her, had the audacity to flirt with her, and this riled him to no end. Whenever Rubio spoke to Helen, Smith felt as if he defiled her sanctity to pollute the purity of her essence.

Strangely, no one knew anything about her. She was a complete enigma. Some said she was a whore from South America, and others said she had once served as a mother superior in some hidden Latin American convent. Her accent was Spanish, but the dialect was indistinct. Among Spanish speakers, she preferred to speak English whenever possible. During their casual conversation, she never answered Smith's personal inquiries. In fact, contrary to his own good judgment, he offered her his own personal history as barter.

"Oh. You would love Puccini when Tosca sings *Vissi d'arte*," Smith cooed.

He began to whistle the aria, but the holiday music drowned him out. Helen began to giggle and quickly buried her mouth in her drink.

"Oh. She sings the beauty of love," he added desperately. "A woman with fine soul. A splendid woman who lives for art."

Helen made eye contact with Smith and giggled again. "I like that," she admitted and placed her forefinger on her lips. "I must see this opera."

A burst of emotion shot through Smith, and he felt his body quiver. Trying to repress his accelerating adrenalin, Smith focused on one idea. "In the spring," he stuttered. "I promise, if you would join me?"

He began to choke and took a hard swallow of wine to silence a rising guttural eruption of nervous phlegm. "Excuse me," he apologized.

"What's your number?" Helen ignored Smith's nervous demeanor.

Smith timidly extracted his smartphone, and she synchronized them. The Bluetooth connection sent him her number. Delighted, he read it and instantly shoved the phone into his clip. "Call me after the holidays," she spoke casually, rotating her finger again around the glass rim. "We can talk after the break, and you can tell me about opera?"

"I can tell you now!" Smith shouted over the din, but a slap on his shoulder interrupted him.

"Smith," Rubio clamored, "Vega called you."

Love turned into fury. Peeved and flummoxed, Smith faced his nemesis with renewed abhorrence.

"Happy Holidays," Rubio warmly wished him and gave him his gift. "I don't like classical music, but I'll give this a try."

Smith instinctively took it and silently held it up at eye level.

"Someone else was my secret Santa," Rubio generously explained. "But everyone gets something from me this year." Confused, Smith could do nothing more than to force a grin and nod his head, "Have a nice rest this vacation," Rubio wished him and then leaned over to kiss Helen on the cheek.

Rubio sauntered away and kissed the other female janitors and maintenance workers who stood nearby. Avoiding physical contact with Kiki, he only waved to her. Helen followed Rubio with her eyes and lost interest in her conversation with Smith.

"The beautiful Miss Helen," Vega shouted. A warm reception of applauses and cheers invited her to come forward to receive her gift.

"I forgot my gift," she said, embarrassed, and walked away, leaving her drink in Smith's empty hand. Smith watched her rush to Vega who handed her a small gift.

"Who's your Santa?" Kiki invaded Smith's private space.

"Ah," Smith thought for a long time. "Rubio."

"Rubio?" Kiki exclaimed. "Shit! What did you get for him?"

"Music," Smith answered numbly. "Opera."

"Shit!" Kiki dismissed Smith's effort. "Who listens to opera?"

"I do," Smith responded and walked out of the restaurant without exchanging a word with anyone. He did not even wish to see Helen, especially after Rubio landed a kiss on her cheek. He—an honorable man—never even touched the woman, but Rubio had the audacity to kiss her.

Sitting alone with his smartphone in his room, Helen's phone number blinked brightly on the screen before fading to sleep mode. Smith looked at Rubio's gift and cursed. He refused to open the box and pushed it away. Miserable, he sought his only escape and began to listen to Rossini's *Largo al Factotum*.

———————

Sinclair studied Sanchez's gift and recalled his Santa exchange decades ago, when Sophie had given him a gift, loosely wrapped in a red velvety cloth.

"What's this?" he asked, not being able to determine its shape. The unorthodox wrapping added to the mystery.

"Open," she purred. Carefully, he unfolded the cloth to reveal a small guitar. "A cavaquinho," she told him proudly. "You will play it and remember me when I go home." Sinclair held up the instrument and gently turned it over, while admiring the fine artisanship and delicate strings.

"I can't play anything," he regretfully explained. "I can't read music."

"Nah," she dismissed his objection. Sitting next to him, Sophie took the cavaquinho, firmly placed her fingers on the strings, and showed him several chords. "Do this," she taught him.

She repeated the action, and a fine, Brazilian sound of a samba came from the stringed instrument. Suddenly halting her performance, she handed the cavaquinho to him. "Now," Sophie ordered him.

Sinclair apprehensively took the cavaquinho in his hands and awkwardly tried to imitate her. Patiently, she gently maneuvered his fingers, and with a cacophonous strum he played three atrocious notes.

Sophie burst out laughing. "I'll make you a Brazilian," she predicted. They spent a couple of hours practicing together, and Sinclair managed, finally, to play a couple of decent chords of a popular bossa nova song.

At home now, he walked to his closet and pulled out the old cavaquinho. Recalling his lesson, he dryly ran through the chords, and after a half hour he once again played the long forgotten jingle. No gift had ever surpassed the cavaquinho, the music, and Sophie's warm tropical smile. Alone for the holiday, he let the echoes of his past Brazilian happiness carry him into a new year once more.

After she had departed for Brazil, he'd learned that she had taught him to play "Desafinado."

How apropos!

Chapter 12

January 2034
Sinclair

"Wait . . . I will remember!"
—Fernando Smith (The Janitor)

Early in January, a major earthquake struck a nearby country that had long suffered from poverty, ignorance, and disease. Most students and faculty did not hear about the catastrophe until they arrived home. The terrible consequences of the human tragedy were ruminated for hours on the Internet and by media sources. The next day Sinclair arrived at school and received an urgent e-mail requesting that he accompany his club representatives to a leadership meeting in the afternoon.

Having Sanchez available to cover his class, Sinclair searched the hallways and classrooms for Asma who had unexpectedly vanished from the building. He hoped she did not skip her classes and create an additional issue for Stile to cite during the afternoon meeting. He checked with some of her friends, but he still failed to find her. Surprisingly, he stumbled upon Smith who was diligently moving a dust brush over the floorboards.

"Señor Smith," Sinclair called his attention.

Smith looked up with a glazed, placid expression.

"You all right?" Sinclair inquired in a calm voice.

He suddenly beamed with joy. "Listen," Smith said and paused to think. Sinclair began to feel a little uneasy. "I am a fortunate man," he revealed, holding up his brush like a baton.

"Oh?' responded Sinclair, curious. He did not wish to hinder Smith's candidness.

"You see," Smith continued, waving the brush. Speckles of dust danced in the air, and some dangled in midair before making a long, leisurely descent onto the carpet below. Others, reluctantly, took a reverse direction. Sinclair watched a mote rotate and float upward before disappearing in the light. "I have a letter confirming my acceptance," Smith said with satisfaction.

"Good?" Sinclair felt relieved, not understanding the full impact behind the meaning of Smith's words. "Rehabilitation? Right?"

"Of course," he expressed impatiently. "The fucker finally sent the recommendation. I have an acceptance letter. It's confirmed."

"Great," Sinclair said and shook Smith's hand. He wanted to leave and continue his search for Asma, so he pulled away, but then he stopped to face Smith again. "Fernando?" Sinclair inquired. "I wanted to . . ." he stuttered.

"Let me say," Smith began to digress in his thoughts and interrupted Sinclair. "A man needs more than a job. You know. You are a man of the world."

Smith's words gave Sinclair pause. "Yes," Sinclair tried to be conciliatory. "I wanted to know if you saw . . ."

"You know," he interrupted again. "A man needs a partner . . . a mate . . . a companion. Life is a long road for people now. We now have two lives. It's all this science and technology stuff. Right? You can't go it alone."

"OK," Sinclair uttered, not understanding Smith's allusion. He began to think that Smith would lose himself in a long, philosophical litany.

"A man," he continued, "needs a woman. A *mujer*."

"Ah," Sinclair accepted his conclusion.

"If you belong to the other side . . . you need a special friend, too. No?" he hastily added. "Like that young hombre . . . Sanchez?"

"Yes," Sinclair followed his thoughts. He was afraid to ask the obvious questions that came to mind.

Without knowing his thoughts, Smith answered anyway. "I think I found my woman," he proudly declared, while releasing more speckles of dust for the unlucky allergy-prone students who lurked in the hallways. "But she needs some . . . refinement."

"Right?" Sinclair continued to be pleasant. "I need you . . ."

"Wait," Smith cut him off. "I need your advice, my friend. This is important stuff for me to consider."

"It is," Sinclair conceded happily, discovering an opportunity to escape the conversation. "And it must be talked about in a more . . . private place. No?"

"Oh?" Smith pondered, holding the brush up to his chin as he mused over Sinclair's suggestion. "You're *justo*. We'll talk later . . . when we can be more private, sí?"

Taking the cue, Sinclair almost darted away until he remembered his dilemma, "Did you see Asma?" Sinclair asked finally.

"Asma?" he answered, confused. "She is not . . ." He laughed to himself and then waved the brush in front of Sinclair's face. "Sorry," he apologized. "I no see her today. Sorry."

"OK," Sinclair said. Determined to make a concerted search for his student, he walked away from Smith after again shaking his hand. "Got to go. Thanks, Fernando."

As Sinclair prepared to rush off, Smith stopped him once more in his tracks. "Don't you want to know who my new friend is?" he called out.

Sinclair abruptly turned around. The identity of Smith's current paramour, whether real or imaginary, never crossed his mind. Deep down, he believed the information ultimately would not be beneficial; however, he replied with a wide, good-natured smile, "Why, yes, . . . yes, of course."

Smith let the brush fall to his side and approached him. He leaned forward and whispered the name into his left ear. "Helen," Smith told him proudly and leaned back, again holding the brush up to his face.

"Classic," Sinclair told him as he tried to place the name with the face.

"She works here," Smith said. "She will share the opera with me. Puccini!"

"I see," Sinclair graciously accepted the confidence. He still could not recall Helen. Feeling embarrassed, he repeated his earlier comment before departing

"Classic," he said. "She launched a thousand ships."

"Ships?" Smith, taken by his own sphere of rapture, inquired. "Like a conquistador?"

"Later. I must look for Asma," Sinclair promised as he bolted around the corner. He told himself that he would have to find out more about Helen before speaking to Smith. Stepping out of the building, he encountered Asma immediately.

"Where were you?" he asked exasperatedly.

"I had to see the Assistant Principal," she declared, holding a tablet in her hands.

"We have a meeting," Sinclair reminded her. "You and the VP have to be there. It's about the quake."

"I heard," Asma responded evasively.

He studied her body language as she blinked several times.

"What's up?" he demanded to know.

Asma looked away from Sinclair and at her tablet.

"Stile?" He made an educated guess.

"What else?" she concurred scornfully.

"Why?" he pressed, afraid of her answer.

"Well," she looked away and pivoted.

Sinclair tapped her authoritatively on the arm. "No," he objected to her moving away. "Let me have it. I'll have to deal with it sooner or later."

Asma looked away as she began explaining the situation. "The First, . . . " she hedged.

"First Priority," he clarified. "The Christian Club? Right?"

"Yeah," Asma confirmed.

"Go on," he urged her.

"Someone offered to debate them," she began. Asma made eye contact with Sinclair who anxiously awaited the whole story.

"Someone?" he probed.

"Yeah," she continued, still trying to avoid Sinclair's questioning.

"It came from them?" he asked, confused. "Originally?"

"They came to us first," she apologized. "I told Mr. Stile."

"So they came to you," he repeated.

They both stopped speaking when two staff members passed by; they waited for them to disappear before continuing.

"We agreed," she emphasized in a more subdued tone. "Then . . . Mr. Stile approached me and said that he won't allow a debate."

"Won't?" he questioned, searching his memory for rules that may have supported Stile's position. "I can't think why not."

"That's what pissed me off!" she almost shouted peevishly. Her dark skin began to show a blush. "It's arbitrary."

"Maybe . . . " he considered and thought over the many reasons why Stile would have justification to cancel the debate. "Maybe not. I'll look into it. Be cool and polite."

"Do I have a choice?" she demanded to know.

"Yes. Do what's smart. Got it?" he reminded her in a cautionary tone.

Asma rejected his response and left in a huff.

"Asma!" he called her. She stopped and impatiently stared at him.

"I bet you would relish a debate," Sinclair teased her. He gave her his best disarming smile.

Slowly, like a melting crayon on a hot range, Asma's anger vanished, and a wide grin appeared. She agreeably waved and walked away.

"That's the Asma," Smith spoke from behind Sinclair.

"Uh?" Sinclair answered, lost in his thoughts. "Yeah."

Smith added, "I found her for you."

"Good man," Sinclair scornfully thanked him. "I got to go."

"Adios," he said, "mi amigo!"

"OK," Sinclair returned.

He critically observed Smith who shuffled off to his cleaning assignment.

The janitor began to sing in Spanish, as he listened to his iPod while moving his brush in a circular motion—still cleaning the recently dusted sideboards.

"He's really wacked," Sinclair concluded uneasily. He walked into his room and caught Sanchez's attention. The students immersed themselves in virtual assignments. "Everything OK?" Sinclair asked.

"Yeah," Sanchez answered pleasantly. "Someone was looking for you."

"Asma?" he wrongly concluded. Sanchez pointed behind Sinclair. When he turned around, he saw Stile.

"Let's speak outside," Stile invited. He led the way, and when Stile was out of view, Sanchez gave Sinclair a thumbs-up. Once they were outside the building's portal, Stile faced Sinclair and began to berate him.

"Look," Stile boldly stated. "I think Asma might have told you about the debate."

"Sure," Sinclair smugly admitted, waiting for the torrential attack of words. "Just a couple of minutes ago."

"Well," Stile continued without skipping a beat, "I am against it."

"OK," Sinclair replied, trying to remain reasonable, as he strategized his next words and actions. He began to fantasize about taking Smith's brush and violently shoving it up Stile's posterior. "But I can't," he admitted. "Too bad," he thought to himself.

"I'm still against the debate," Stile clarified, shaking his head. "But after speaking to Dr. Pierce, I cannot impede the students' freedom of speech. I didn't want to have those Christian kids face skepticism and doubt—especially in our world that's filled with so little belief."

"Well," Sinclair interjected. "At least the belief in the right to free speech is alive." He gave him a wide, affable smile. Stile did not return the conciliatory gesture as he continued to vent his agitation.

"I'll send an e-mail about scheduling the debate," he added reluctantly.

"I think we should let the club presidents set the date," Sinclair suggested. "With your consent."

"Fine," Stile conceded and stormed away from the building. Sinclair watched him hurriedly vacate the area.

"I saw him first," Smith said from behind. Sinclair turned around to see the janitor still holding his dust brush. "He was looking for you," Smith finished his thoughts.

"Good," Sinclair accepted his observation. "Next time let me know sooner!" He snatched the brush out of Smith's hand. Startled, Smith silently gaped. "Have this in a safe place. I might need it."

"You know," Smith spoke, relaxing and returning to his senses. "In life you must either find the truth, or it finds you. Sometimes the same goes for people."

"Good advice," Sinclair answered. He returned the dust brush and walked inside, leaving Smith confused in his wake.

"The man needs a rest," Smith concluded alone. "Too much *tormento*. Problems. Like me. Very bad." He lifted up the brush and made a note to follow Sinclair's directive and store it safely in a secure place.

Chapter 13

January 2034
Sanchez

Alone in the virtual instruction laboratory, Sanchez followed protocol by categorizing and securing each tablet and computer for evening storage. He scanned the machines against the students' identification numbers and verified that 100 percent of the students had complied with the rules of usage. They always did—which bored him. Since September, he had had predictable and bland days. Worst of all, Sanchez had little or no interaction with the students; he was only a proctor and not an official teacher.

The day ended, and he waited for Sinclair to visit and talk to him about his request to teach a class. So far the paperwork had traveled through the bureaucratic machinations of the university and the district. After the winter break, he had been told he could call upon a district contact to facilitate the process. Pierce volunteered his help, too. No one wanted to lose Sanchez to another profession as so few young people opted to teach.

Sanchez's phone unpredictably vibrated, and he read the text message announcement:

Our institution is pleased to tentatively recommend you for admission to law school during the fall semester of 2034. Be assured that you will . . .

Sanchez stopped reading the e-mail when Sinclair walked into the lab.

"Everything OK?" he asked. "You look upset."

Sanchez continued to glance at the message before rapidly shoving the phone into his holster. "Fine," he waved off Sinclair's concerns. "Any news?"

"We are officially cleared for the lecture," Sinclair declared. He conveyed his pleasure by sticking out his hand for a high five. Sanchez, confused, reciprocated without any enthusiasm. "I thought you would be happy." Sinclair remarked, disappointed.

"I am," Sanchez lied, trying to resurrect a cheerful disposition.

"OK? Tell me what's going on."

Sanchez looked away and then exhaled heavily. "I don't know," he admitted his dilemma. "Same stuff with my partner. I got an offer."

"Law school?" Sinclair assumed anxiously. He waited patiently for Sanchez to continue, but then Asma stuck her head into the laboratory.

"Mr. Sinclair!" she shouted. Disconcerted, they both looked up to witness Asma enter the lab with a little dance step. "We're good to go," she announced proudly. "I already got my notes."

"Exciting," Sinclair told her and clapped his hands.

"Good job!" Sanchez congratulated her and temporarily forgot his own dilemma. "Why?"

"Why?" she retorted indignantly.

Sinclair shot an astonished stare at Sanchez.

"Oh," Sanchez recovered his thoughts. "I heard about the debate. Good job, again."

His recovery did not seem to appease her. She looked deflated. "I'll send you the details," she promised.

"Lots of details," Sinclair reminded her. "And I need the other sponsor to confirm all this. Can I trust it to you?"

"You have to ask?" she countered and disappeared again into the hallway.

"Is she always like that?" Sanchez inquired.

"That's when she's happy," Sinclair pointed out. "You should see her when she's upset." Sinclair growled as an example.

"Ha!" Sanchez laughed. "I remember the float for homecoming." He chuckled to himself and looked down, recalling his dialogue with Asma a couple of months earlier. "I can't wait until I can lecture," he admitted. "I need it to round things out for me."

"Well," Sinclair offered him a reprieve. "Don't make a rash decision until you do. You can't know unless you try. At least the law school offer gives you another option, if the lecturing bombs for you."

Sanchez reflected on the advice for a moment and nodded his head. "Right," he agreed timidly, afraid what Nick would say if he savored the lecture and completely fell in love with teaching. "At least it will be fun."

"We have to work on a lesson plan," Sinclair reminded him of the tedious aspects of the job. "It's not all glory. A lot of it is preparation."

"I have to see more of what you're doing," Sanchez committed himself.

"We'll talk later," Sinclair assured him and looked in the direction where Asma ran off. "I better follow her trail and make sure she doesn't gum up the works."

"What?" Sanchez asked in confusion. "Oh? I get it."

"Old school," Sinclair amiably corrected himself. "She doesn't nuke it."

"That's what I thought," Sanchez concurred and gave Sinclair a warm grin.

Smiling, Sinclair mockingly saluted Sanchez and followed Asma out of the building.

Once Sanchez felt that Sinclair had safely left the building, he called Nick.

"You got it?" Nick asked without any prompting.

Sanchez became irritated. "How did you know?" he questioned.

"I told you before," Nick answered evasively. "I have the right friend in the right place."

"This is bullshit," Sanchez raised his voice. Nick did not react, and Sanchez could only listen to silence. "Nick!" he called out into the phone's speaker.

"Go ahead," Nick mockingly recommended. "Try on your lecturing. See if it fits, and then you can decide. All I got to say is that I won't be here if you want to play the schoolmarm." Abruptly, the phone went silent.

"Bitch," Sanchez cursed and began to feel like crying. "Shit." He quietly examined his options and could not foresee losing Nick from his life. Secretly, Sanchez knew that he was postponing the inevitable. Some loss was inevitable. Sadly, he felt he would choose teaching over law, along with the unpleasant consequences.

"Hey," Asma stuck her head in the door. Trying to compose himself, Sanchez lifted himself up in his chair and smiled.

"Sinclair is looking for you," Sanchez warned her. "He went that way."

"I had to talk to some people," Asma explained. "So I went around."

"Yeah?" he asked. "What's up?"

Asma coyly looked at him and offered her most friendly, seductive grin. "You want to be one of the judges?" she asked bashfully.

"For the debate?" Sanchez asked, pulling his thoughts away from law school and Nick.

Asma nodded and elevated herself on the balls of her feet, like a dog begging for a morsel of food.

"Sure," Sanchez agreed. "No problem."

"All right," Asma punched the air and jumped up. "This is going to be so cool. You'll see. We're having three judges. It'll be an in-house thing." Asma waved to him and dashed off.

He returned to his text message and read the rest of it, taking note of the deadline for him to respond officially. Fortunately, it came after the lecture date. Sanchez sat silently as he thought alone, when all of a sudden the music from a Wagnerian opera floated into the lab. From the janitor's closet, Smith was playing Siegfried's *Funeral March*. The music began to swell and trumpet with its famous leitmotif of noble death.

"How appropriate," Sanchez concluded and shut down his computer, ending his session for the day.

January Intermission

Sinclair accepted Laura's invitation and paid a visit to her lawyer.

The lawyer—a Mr. G—would not provide his full name and insisted that they meet in a small diner in a small desert town outside Los Angeles. Following the handwritten directions he found in his school mailbox—which Sinclair believed Laura had provided, he arrived ahead of schedule and sat in a booth, facing the door. When Mr. G entered the diner, Sinclair immediately recognized him despite his blue-collar clothes. He was wearing a pair of dirty Levis, a plaid shirt, work boots, and a trucker's baseball cap. Mr. G appeared to be a trucker, but his gait gave him away. He walked towards Sinclair with the confidence and grace of a successful trial lawyer who had years of experience strutting in front of a skeptical jury. He sat silently in front of Sinclair and expressed nothing, except a nod. Under the hat, Sinclair saw a soft, pudgy man with brown eyes and graying blond hair. He smoked a black e-cigarette that released an innocuous blue vapor. Hanging from a red lanyard, it rested on his chest when not in use.

"What would you like?" a redheaded server asked, wearing the traditional attire of the diner: a blue dress, tennis shoes, and a ketchup-stained white blouse. Unlike bygone eras, she carried a tablet, instead of a notepad and pencil.

"Coffee," Mr. G said rapidly, "and a club sandwich."

"You?" she addressed Sinclair.

"Coffee," Sinclair answered and looked at Mr. G.

"Try the club," Mr. G encouraged him. "It's good."

"It has no cholesterol," the server assured Sinclair, "and low calories."

"OK," Sinclair accepted amiably.

Mr. G expressed his approval with another nod and remained silent, continuing to puff on his e-cigarette. A few moments later, the server brought the coffee, along with sweeteners and creamer. Mr. G poured a packet of the blue sweetener into his coffee and a touch of nonfat cream. "Coffee is good," Mr. G confirmed cheerfully. He took a long sip.

Sinclair poured some creamer into his coffee and took a sip after Mr. G put down his cup. "Laura's friend," Mr. G broke the ice. "That's what I'll call you, friend."

"Fine," Sinclair accepted politely and took another sip. "You'll be G."

Mr. G accepted the salutation and took another drink of his coffee. "Just like the old days," Mr. G expressed with gustatory satisfaction. "Wait until we have the sandwich. Eat first, and then we'll talk."

Sinclair silently agreed to the conditions and finished his first cup of coffee. The waitress arrived with more coffee, and later she brought the two men their sandwiches. They both ate quietly, relishing every bite. Sinclair finished three cups of coffee, and he was gripping the fourth cup when the server removed their plates.

"You're right," Sinclair told him. "It was good."

"I'm glad. We can now talk," Mr. G concluded, holding up his coffee. "Good?"

"Great," Sinclair agreed and took a sip. "Don't you think we should be careful?"

"No one is here," Mr. G assured him and took another nicotine puff from his e-cigarette. Sinclair made a visual assessment and realized that no one had entered the restaurant since both men arrived. Mr. G responded to his silent query. "I have my arrangements," Mr. G confided. "We can talk."

"Can we?" Sinclair had his doubts. He instinctively understood that Mr. G would not reveal the details of those arrangements. "How can I be sure?"

"Laura," he reminded him. "And this!"

"I don't like this cloak-and-dagger bullshit!" Sinclair said, frustrated.

Mr. G pulled a small tablet from the jacket and slid it across the table. "Go ahead," he encouraged him. "Look it over. But we don't have all night."

Sinclair made a perfunctory examination of the tablet's contents and saw that Mr. G had all of his government documents, including Vega's private notes. All were confidentially coded. "I guess I can't ask you?" Sinclair spoke the obvious.

"No," Mr. G regretfully shook his head. "But I can tell you some things right off." The very tone of his words caused Sinclair to flinch. "First," Mr. G explained with some interspersed facts. "Your sabbatical is a farce."

"OK?" he absorbed the information, while holding down his anger.

"If you don't take your assignment," Mr. G added, puffing on his e-cigarette, "they will order you to take any assignment of their choice a week after you retire."

"Under what pretense?" Sinclair demanded to know. The coffee began to sour in his stomach

"They don't have to use a pretense," Mr. G reminded Sinclair of the power of the Rehabilitation Department. "You are a cog to serve the state. They can't have a loose cannon. Listen, you can be denied rehabilitation."

"Denied?" he questioned, not believing what he heard. "How? It's my right."

"Rights?" Mr. G scoffed and began to chuckle. "You have no rights. The Rehabilitation Act and new genetic treatments suspended your constitutional rights. I won't get into the minutia, but you are 'the property of the state' once you retire. They can decide on your behalf. They have the power of attorney. You only have a right to die. You should have known better. . . . you're a social science teacher."

The word *they* began to have cynical overtones. "Then why bother with the sabbatical for a year?" Sinclair asked for more clarity. "Why even offer it?"

"You don't get it?" Mr. G spoke lamentably and finished his coffee. Sinclair let the rest of his sit on the table. "You are being provided an opportunity to leave the spotlight," Mr. G explained as if he were speaking to a pupil. "Once you are out of the workforce, then the legal manipulations can come into play. It's very subtle, Machiavellian, and effective. When it happens, it will seem completely rational and legal. You won't be able to see the forest for the trees."

"They want to have me placed where they need me," Sinclair surmised.

"Yes," Mr. G spoke with satisfaction and gave him a congratulatory grin. "If you fail—either by lack of skills or resistance—you will die in due time. Finis. That's it. They can't waste time with useless cogs."

"Useless cogs?" Sinclair resented the allusion.

"No," Mr. G simplified, "you're not, . . . but a sabbatical will make you one. You need to rescind your request before retirement. You still have a few months."

"So I take my assignment and spend the next eighty years as a useful cog?" Sinclair sarcastically concluded.

"Or die," Mr. G factually added.

"So you're telling me some people will be given rehabilitation only to have it rescinded," Sinclair sought clarification. "Because they don't need them."

"That's the beauty of it all," Mr. G explained poetically. "Necessity supersedes value. You still have value if you want more time. Take it, . . . if you don't, well . . . "

"Why did Laura tell me about the sabbatical?" Sinclair stopped him.

"She was misinformed, too," Mr. G answered quickly and seemed to become a little edgy.

"Why are you telling me this?" he naively asked.

Mr. G made eye contact with Sinclair and spoke in a clear voice. "You and Laura are my case personnel," Mr. G revealed. "I don't want useful lives wasted. We never met. . . . Good-bye." He stuck the e-cigarette in his mouth and exhaled a large, blue ring of vapor in Sinclair's direction.

"And what if I talk?" he threatened. "You know?"

Mr. G guffawed. "You can answer that for yourself," he reminded Sinclair of his political impotence. "You're too smart to ignore the obvious consequences."

"People talked about stuff in the past," Sinclair challenged him. "It changed things."

"Change?" Mr. G contemplated. "Never a real change--Good luck,"

He walked off, never looking back at Sinclair. When he stepped out of the diner, the waitress reappeared and began to add packaged sweeteners and ketchup bottles to the table containers. Customers began to drift in, and the restaurant business quickly picked up.

From Sinclair's perspective, the abnormal had become the new norm.

It is not every day that someone paid attention to Smith.

Today, with the confidence of his legal rights, Smith entered an office at the Federal Retirement Rehabilitation Center with his papers and documents in hand. Unlike most people, Smith relished the tactile sensation of paper. Slightly anxious, he sat in a Spartan room with a single desk and a computer tablet. Across from him hung a monitor with a man's face, displaying insipid features and vacant eyes. The man glared at Smith with aloof contempt.

"I am here to pick my profession," Smith announced, not waiting for the official introductions.

He held up his documents and waved them in front of the monitor, briefly suspending the papers in front of the nameless official. "We have several more requirements," the man droned. "Mr. Fernando Smith?"

Smith gulped and dropped his hands and documents to his lap. Furious, he began to imagine that Rubio had sabotaged his application. "My employer submitted the paperwork?" Smith probed and took a long breath, as he anticipated the worst possible news.

"You must continue to complete the process," the man added scornfully. When he spoke, the man's mouth moved, but his facial muscles remained stiff and plastic. Smith, puzzled, took a few moments to realize that the man on the monitor's screen was some sort of a simulation, a virtual representation of a federal employee.

"Why am I talking to a robot?" Smith demanded to know. The man's face became inert. "Why are you wasting my time?" Smith continued to castigate the simulation.

More silence followed. "Anyone home?" Smith continued to demand an answer and gruffly stood up.

"Sit down!" the lips spat out. Shaken, Smith collapsed in his seat. The documents fell on the floor. "Fill out the official survey on the tablet," the lips ordered, "You will be contacted later."

"What?" he answered, confused, and looked at the tablet on the desk. The monitor then went blank.

"Qué? Smith asked in Spanish. "¡No me diga! Don't do this!" He then reluctantly picked up the tablet and tapped the "I Agree" icon. The screen lit up, and a survey posted several questions. "Read the questions," Smith read the instructions to himself, "and answer them all."

He scrutinized the questions and then read them over again aloud. "Are you tired? Do you have a sex drive? Are you in a relationship? Is it difficult to remember the last time you were happy? Do you avoid dealing with other people?" He finished reading.

Smith stood up and slammed the tablet on the desk. "I'm avoiding talking to you!" he declared. "Next time . . . you talk to my lawyer. Maricón! Bastard! Have a good fucking day!" Smith spat out more epithets in Spanish, picked up his documents, and bolted out of the office, slamming the door behind him.

"Good day," the nameless, ghostly simulation responded.

Chapter 14

February 2034
Sanchez

"Don't go away . . . por favor."
—Fernando Smith (The Janitor)

The special day approached.

After preparing for weeks, Sanchez stood in front of Sinclair's history class. The lesson plans had assembled themselves in piecemeal fashion, according to the state's core curriculum, and with Sinclair's input, Sanchez created a lecture that embellished the unit without violating the pacing guide for the course. Unlike the days when Sinclair first taught high school, instructors were not allowed to improvise or substitute material since students faced a mandatory end-of-the-year examination that was based on the curriculum.

"Look," Sinclair carefully explained, "we have to file and submit your lecture. So, . . . I waited for several breaks in the course where you can expand on the topic."

"Expand?" Sanchez questioned skeptically. "I have to follow the standards."

"Yes and no," Sinclair responded mischievously and averted his eyes. "Your lecture has to touch on the subject matter, but you don't have to follow it slavishly . . . verbatim. Got it?"

"I think?" Sanchez was not convinced.

"I'll give you some choices, and we can go from there," Sinclair said, as he searched the core curriculum for places where Sanchez could embellish on the material. "Here are some place markers I created. The board should approve."

Sanchez searched through the topics and picked one that he thought he could address and make an impact by borrowing from sources that would be unfamiliar to the students. "Let's go with that one," he decided, pointing to a notation.

Sinclair examined the choice and approved enthusiastically. "This is a good one," he said, adding, "You keep the details to yourself. OK?"

Sanchez grinned and then took the paperwork out of his hand. He began to plan a surprise. "It will be a surprise to the kids," Sanchez assured Sinclair, "and to you. I hope you'll like it."

"I'm sure," Sinclair acknowledged quizzically. "This will be fine. They can't object."

"I hope not," Sanchez responded. He began to have his doubts about the administration.

"Leave it to me," Sinclair said, guaranteeing its acceptability. Despite Sanchez's neophyte apprehension, Sinclair came through. The administration approved the proposal, and Sanchez had a date.

In the days leading up to the lecture, Nick took a trip at the request of Sanchez, who wanted to avoid any argument or distraction. He remained alone for two days. Where Nick stayed, Sanchez did not know. Nevertheless, the respite provided him a peaceful atmosphere in which to concentrate. Finally, the day arrived.

"Ready to go?" Sinclair interrupted Sanchez's thought process when they entered the classroom.

"Yeah," Sanchez answered nervously, holding his tablet and a black portfolio bag that he placed at his feet.

The students wandered in with their tablets, logged into the school's website and into the portal. Sanchez uploaded his notes and PowerPoint slides for them, including his video presentations. Muffled side conversations and curious stares added to the suppressed anxiety of each student who were waiting to listen to the new, young lecturer. Although Sanchez tried to eavesdrop on their conversations, he worked avidly all the while on his tablet, and he could not discern any comments about himself or the upcoming presentation.

"They like you," Sinclair told him, knowing how he felt. "Be yourself. I'm looking forward to it, too."

His support lifted Sanchez's spirits as Pierce entered the room. The students' conversations ceased.

"Hello," Pierce greeted everyone and made eye contact with Sanchez. "We're all lucky to have Mr. Sanchez, and I look forward to his lecture today. Let's show our appreciation."

The students hesitantly followed Pierce's lead and began to applaud. Sanchez bowed slightly and projected an uneasy smile at Pierce and the students.

"No pressure," Sinclair joked. "I didn't know."

Sanchez, with a trickle of perspiration dripping under his armpits, felt a warm flush spread across his face and throughout his body.

"Relax," Sinclair advised him, seeing Sanchez blush.

The applause stopped, and Sanchez forced himself to begin the lecture. He took a traditional approach. "Mr. Pierce," Sanchez began his lecture, "Mr. Sinclair, and students, . . . I welcome you to my first school lecture. Thank you for this opportunity to speak to you."

Again, there was another round of applause, but this time the students showed more enthusiasm and carried on—to Pierce's displeasure—for several long moments. Sanchez raised his hands to silence them, and they quietly adopted a façade of academic reservation, interspersed with whispered undertones.

"Hitler," Sanchez bluntly stated. The room became intensely silent. "When someone uses the word, the effect is chilling." Everyone stared intently at Sanchez. Pierce shifted his posture, and Sinclair panned his eyes across the class.

"Cancer, Rape. Hate. Racism. Murder. . . words . . . words that hurt!" Sanchez spat out in rapid succession. Sanchez paused and focused his attention on Pierce who shifted again. "Hitler," Sanchez repeated deliberately. "To misquote a famous U.S. President . . . a name that will live in infamy."

"Even in the twenty-first century, we live on a planet that still experiences the horrible repercussions of Hitler's actions," Sanchez reminded his audience. "His name holds deadly and unspeakable memories!" He continued to hold his attention on Pierce, who appeared to wilt slightly under his gaze.

"But a fear of a name," Sanchez quickly continued, "is useless. In reality, Hitler's crimes were no more evil or despicable than Attila the Hun and other evil despots. But we don't feel like losing our lunch when we hear old Attila's name, do we?"

A nervous laugh resonated. "But Hitler can't be allowed to be the boogeyman," Sanchez interjected. More giggles echoed. "I won't look for the *Hitlerman* boogeyman under my bed," Sanchez mused and heard more giggles. "He isn't hiding in the closet, . . . but I fear his memory."

The attentive silence returned. "Like every fear," Sanchez pressed on and shot a glance at Sinclair, "every monster, when it's understood, loses its psychological control over us." Some of the students nodded agreeably. Pierce began to relax.

"So," Sanchez concluded emphatically, "we have to kill the monster, but let's first try to understand how he came to power. Can anyone tell me?"

He suddenly recognized Asma sitting in the second row. Sanchez looked at Asma who had shown a visible unwillingness to speak, thanks to Sinclair's earlier coaching. But now she raised her hand.

"All right," Sanchez acknowledged her calmly.

"Hitler received money from powerful corporations," Asma volunteered.

"The Weimar Constitution failed," another student added. "The old government gave in and collapsed."

"He had a scapegoat everyone could blame," one more student suggested. "The Jews."

"Propaganda," a student shouted.

"And attacks on other parties," a student yelled from the corner of the room.

Sanchez looked around and studied the group.

"You're all right," he congratulated them. "But you forgot one thing."

No one spoke. Then Asma stood up. Sinclair shook his head.

"OK," she rejected Sinclair's silent admonition, "the man himself." She confidently sat down, and Sanchez smiled.

"The man himself," he repeated. "Historians and witnesses say he had a magnetic power over people. He believed God called on him, and his absolute belief in his vision convinced others of his supernatural calling. The German people had a belief in an idol. A false god, similar to a bad religion, an evil cult out of control." Sanchez waited and made eye contact with Pierce and Sinclair before proceeding. Pierce appeared perplexed.

"Let's hear some examples and see how he pulled it off," Sanchez declared and lifted the remote control from his desktop. The lights dimmed, and the projector began to show black-and-white clips of Hitler's different speeches.

Hitler began to speak to a crowd of government officials:

The struggle for world domination will be fought entirely between us, between Germans and Jews. All else is façade and illusion. Behind England stands Israel, and behind France, and behind the United States. Even when we have driven the Jew out of Germany, he remains our world enemy.

In the next scene, he shouted to a room of party followers:

They refer to me as an uneducated barbarian. Yes, we are barbarians. We want to be barbarians; it is an honored title to us. We shall rejuvenate the world. This world is near its end.

In another scene, Hitler shouted again:

Providence has ordained that I should be the greatest liberator of humanity. I am freeing man from the restraints of an intelligence that has taken charge, from the dirty and degrading self-mortification of a false vision called conscience and morality, and from the demands of a freedom and independence which only a very few can bear.

Towards the end of the speech, he concluded with the following:

. . . Do you now appreciate the depth of our National Socialist Movement? Can there be anything greater and more all comprehending? Those who see in National Socialism nothing more than a political movement know scarcely anything of it. It is more even than religion; it is the will to create humankind anew.

The lights brightened slowly, and Sanchez turned back to the class and slowly faced them. He looked down at his tablet. "What can you say about Hitler's themes?" he queried in a low-pitched voice.

The room remained silent, and Asma rose to her feet. "He speaks like the haters from my country," she revealed, unashamed. "They want to reduce people to things . . . to objects. People are the state's tools to be used and to be thrown away. Only the unthinking are welcome to the dictator . . . the authorities will think for you. And if you don't belong, . . . you are dead."

Asma sat down, and every student gawked at her. Pierce approvingly smiled, and Sinclair wrinkled his brow in concern over her histrionics.

"Hate, hate, and more hate," Sanchez repeated, "then slavery and death." Sanchez paused and turned briefly to face the Smart Board.

"There's another vision available to us," Sanchez revealed, as if the information were new. "Someone from this period in history satirized the hater and gave us an alternative: The vision we all would like to really believe in."

Everyone stared and waited. "Do you know who?" Sanchez persisted with his question.

"Churchill?" a student guessed.

"No," Sanchez rejected amiably. "Good guess, though. I have someone else in mind." He looked around and waited before speaking. "Charlie," he enunciated every syllable, "Chaplin."

Most of the students looked dumbfounded. One young man timidly raised his hand. "Is he the funny guy with the mustache in the old black-and-white films?" he asked cautiously.

Sanchez reached down and lifted his bag, as he turned his back to the class. When he faced them again, he wore a square mustache under his lips, a small, black bowler hat, and a retractable hooked cane. He began to rotate the cane and waddle in front of the class, shuffling towards Pierce. When he reached Pierce, Sanchez scornfully bowed to him, dramatically moved his mustache up and down with a quizzical expression, and then returned to his podium, displaying a haughty attitude of humorous contempt. The class erupted, giving him a standing ovation.

"Thank you," Sanchez said humbly and held up the cane, waving it at the students. "Please. Sit." Pierce and Sinclair stood up briefly and cheered along with the students.

"You see," Sanchez continued as the cheers slowly diminished. "Chaplin once said that Hitler imitated his mustache." He heard a small laugh. "So, to return the favor, Chaplin made a movie called *The Great Dictator*. Chaplin played dual roles in the film: a Jewish barber and the dictator. Eventually, they are mistaken for one another, with the dictator arrested, and the Jewish barber mistakenly elevated to the role of the dictator. He plays the role of a barber, and through a case of mistaken identity, he is elevated to the position of the dictator. Also, the brilliance of it all is that Chaplin represents an oppressed minority like the Jews in Hitler's Germany. At the end of the movie, he mocks Hitler's speech with a different version of his diatribe and evil ranting. Let's look at it."

Once more, the lights dimmed, and a few whispers and coughs could be heard. On the screen, Charlie Chaplin, wearing a pseudo-

Nazi uniform labeled with X's instead of swastikas, sits with some cronies and reluctantly decides to give a speech. Despite his apprehensions, he nervously speaks in front of a gathering of citizens and party officials.

The students watched the speech and listened to Chaplin urge his audience to join in a crusade against humanity's enemies: poverty, ignorance, and racism. He calls for humanity to reject political oppression and adopt progress and science to create a better world.

The speech ended with a solitary gasp, followed by whispers and sporadic chatter. Immediately, the light slowly brightened, and Sanchez stood staring at the blank screen. He leisurely turned around to face his audience.

"Didn't he do quiet movies?" a male student asked in an impromptu manner.

The class laughed, and Sanchez smiled benevolently. "Silent movies," he gently corrected him. "Yes, he made silent movies." More snickers could be heard, and even Pierce and Sinclair smiled. "So?" Sanchez explored for a reaction.

A timid young woman raised her hand. "We have ourselves to blame," the young woman began, "and to congratulate. I think Chaplin is saying that our future is our own. We must cherish our humanity and make sure our humanity is kept alive."

"Right," Sanchez congratulated her. "We are not androids with machine minds. We are humans. Hang onto your humanity. That's one of the most important lessons in history. Then we can kill off the Hitler boogeymen of hate and prejudice."

Sanchez paused and made direct eye contact with Pierce. "And I hope to one day present more lessons. Thank you, Director, Mr. Sinclair, and students." Sanchez gave them a deep bow and placing the bowler on his head as he rose.

The students stood up and applauded, cheering and whistling loudly. Pierce walked over to Sanchez to shake his hand, and Sinclair gave him a thumbs-up. A small crowd gathered around Sanchez, and Sinclair silently stepped back and watched.

Chapter 15

After Sanchez's triumphant lecture, Sinclair decided to leave as soon as possible. He took a circuitous route to his house and arrived an hour later than usual. When he parked the car, he admitted to himself that he felt slightly depressed. The emotion, at first, disturbed him for he wondered if he were jealous of Sanchez. Despite the confusing mixture of emotions, he concluded that he felt proud of Sanchez's lecture. It had stimulated the students and haunted them on a level that no one could understand.

When he entered the house, he admitted to one of his emotions—he felt old.

Inside, the house was empty and abandoned. In the garage, a fragmented motorbike sat, waiting for assembly, and many additional parts remained in unopened delivery boxes. At this stage in his life, Sinclair felt he was himself only waiting. The mysterious attorney caused him to assess his options seriously since he still had time to rescind his sabbatical and opt for a better career, one that would guarantee him a comfortable salary and an additional lifetime of memories.

Did he want the additional memories? Or the career? What irritated him was the stark truth that he had no one to share his future, although the odds of finding a new partner, if he would make the effort, were on his side.

Sitting by his computer, he found a message. It asked him to call at a designated hour. He looked at the clock and decided that he would have to call the next morning when they would both be awake.

Fortunately, there was no problem. Her stay in Japan solidified his realization that the marriage was over. He was alone.

———————

Climbing into bed, he was taken again by an eruption of feelings, and he closed his eyes to follow the images that connected the feelings with forgotten memories. When Sanchez gave his lecture, Sinclair began to remember his first year as a teacher in a new school. As he rolled over and drifted to sleep, the dream of his first day of teaching returned.

His students were a group of ESL migrants from many countries, but they primarily had arrived from Mexico and Central America. Unlike Sanchez, he never had the opportunity of lecturing to an advanced class of history students until much later in his career. Although he had a history degree, he took the temporary certification to teach ESL and thereby have employment.

The district assigned him to a distant corner in the northwest hills of the San Fernando Valley where many immigrants settled, looking for jobs on the street and in warehouse parking lots. They sent their children to nearby schools. Unlike the schools in their countries, the American schools were free and functional. His class was tucked in the far north corner of the schoolyard. When he arrived, the principal greeted him and happily shook his hand. The man was tall and lank, with a balding head, hooked nose, and dark, black eyes. His suit was professionally tailored, and it looked like it had been purchased on the fashionable side of Encino.

"Welcome aboard," the principal congratulated him in the middle of the school quad. "I'm Mr. Clark. You are our new breed of teachers."

The word *breed* felt disconcerting to Sinclair.

"We have a new future," he continued to talk without waiting for Sinclair's response. He continued to shake his hand. "You are going to teach the immigrants. This is a nation of immigrants. Maybe one of your students may find the cure to cancer or win the Nobel Prize for Peace."

Sinclair wanted to ask why he could not win the Nobel Prize.

"Yes," the principal finally released his hand. "And you are one of our new emergency teachers."

The words *breed* and *emergency* really did not sit well with Sinclair.

"So the future is all in you," the principal proclaimed. "What an exciting time! I envy your opportunity and adventure." The principal studied Sinclair's face, almost as if he had just realized there was actually a person there listening to him. "Do you have any questions?" he asked.

Sinclair had many but decided to ask only one. "I never taught ESL," he said.

Mr. Clark gave him a puzzled look and then chuckled loudly. "No problem," he triumphantly concluded. "It will be pure. No preconceptions. All natural instinct. Honest teaching."

He continued to chuckle to himself and produced a sheet of paper—slapping it into Sinclair's open palm. The school bell rang, and Mr. Clark left Sinclair alone. Suddenly, he was adrift amid the traffic of students and staff, rushing across the campus towards their classes and offices.

"Where do I go?" Sinclair asked, desperately holding the sheet of paper with one hand and his thin, dilapidated Samsonite briefcase with the other hand. No one answered him, and he looked around and down at the sheet of paper the principal had handed him.

Soon, a middle-aged woman, wearing a long, frock dress and a pair of pink tennis shoes, stopped to speak to him. A long, wooden knitting needle held a bundle of her hair together like a snood. "Lost, young man?" she asked quizzically.

Sinclair just gazed at her hair; he had not heard her question. "What?" he asked, bewildered.

"Lost?" she asked, raising her voice. Instinctively, she took the sheet of paper out of Sinclair's hand and read. "Young man," the woman addressed him, "I'm your department chair."

Caught off guard, Sinclair struggled to respond.

"I'm Ms. Golden," she introduced herself. "You are in the bungalows. Next to Ag field."

"Ag field?" Sinclair inquired.

"It's a small farm," she explained. "Agriculture. Part of our vocational school." Ms. Golden returned the paper to Sinclair who automatically gripped it. "There's a sub there," she added gruffly. "I don't like him."

She appraised his appearance and expressed a moderate amount of satisfaction. "At least you look decent," she complimented weakly.

"Follow me." Sinclair quickly fell into place and strode behind her to cross the emptying quad.

"Mr. Clark never tells me anything," she complained aloud. "They send me teachers, and I have to break them in. We'll meet later in the afternoon to go over lesson plans and the textbook."

Stopping suddenly, she looked directly at him. "If you want to make it," she warned him, "come to my office in Room 10. We have to go over the curriculum guides. The vice principal can be a pain if your lesson plans are screwy or nonexistent." Offering him the obligatory smile, Ms. Golden turned around and continued her march towards the bungalows.

Sinclair passed two buildings before he reached the bungalow areas. Originally designed to be temporary, the first quad's structures, like the others, sat on raised platforms. They were painted a peach color that had long faded in the hot California sun. Each building had wooden floorboards, single-hung sash windows, and open transoms. A large, concrete stoop led to a rickety wooden door with a single brass knob and a deadbolt lock. The stucco around the building had begun to crack and chip, exposing the underlying chicken wire and wooden frame. Sinclair noticed that the date of construction had been stamped into the last step of each bungalow. Ms. Golden watched him reading the dates. She read aloud, ". . . 1954. These are old and should be condemned." Sinclair nodded in agreement and did not notice when Ms. Golden walked away.

"You are coming?" she shouted several yards ahead of him. Sinclair skipped quickly like a tardy pupil trying to catch the bus. He was panting heavily when he caught up to his chairperson. "You need to get into shape," she advised him in a maternal tone.

"Right," Sinclair agreed.

Her stamina was amazing. They passed through two more quads of dilapidated bungalows, and a fetid odor reached Sinclair's nose before he arrived at his destination. "In the back," she abruptly informed him.

They tuned right at the end of a row of bungalows that were sandwiched against a rusting chain-link fence. A small narrow walkway, which ran parallel to the blackened and chipped concrete stoops, allowed the students to enter the bungalows. On the other side of the fence, Sinclair discovered the source of the malodorous stench. He saw several shacks containing every possible farm animal. A few feet away, a cow ate silage from a cracked, sunbaked trough.

"She just got here," Ms. Golden revealed.

"Not only the cow," Sinclair said, pointing to several cow patties that were entertaining swarms of competing flies.

"You get used to it," she assured him.

Sinclair wanted to retort, "I was raised on a farm," but held his tongue along with his breath.

"Over there," she said, pointing finally to the last, hidden bungalow.

"Of course," he muttered as they walked along the edge of the chain-link fence.

Sinclair kept his eyes downcast, trying to avoid any fecal matter that may have wandered onto the pathway. When they reached the stoop, he read the stamped date, "1953."

"These were the first ones," Ms. Golden recounted, like a tour guide walking through Pompeii's ruins. "Lots of history here."

"I can see," Sinclair bemoaned, beginning to doubt his sanity at taking the ESL job.

"Come on up," she urged him as she leaped up the stoop and swung open the door. Sinclair followed her and peered into the murky room. Abruptly, a series of mimicked words in mispronounced accents blasted out of the recesses of another bungalow room.

"I come. You come. He comes," the dissonant voices repeated in deafening discord. "She comes. We come. They come."

Sinclair listened in disbelief. "You coming?" she urged him again, sticking her head out of the dim room.

Sinclair sheepishly entered the bungalow room that would be his classroom for the rest of the school year. He immediately noticed that it was bare. Despite the gloom of the weak incandescent bulbs, strong streaks of sunlight managed to pierce the dusty air through bent venetian blinds that tilted in stoic defiance to time's erosion and neglect. Inside, seven immigrant Mexican and Vietnamese students, spread about the thirty-desk room, sat attentively in iron chairs. Most of the students—a balance of girls and boys—wore threadbare clothes and recycled shoes, given to them by a local charity or church.

Two blackboards, one in the front and another alongside the entrance door opposite the windows and transoms, had been smeared with layers of decades-old yellow chalk dust that had left a permanent stain. Several words, scrawled into the dust, highlighted a confusing vocabulary lesson that had been abandoned either yesterday or thirty years before. An old chiseled and cracked wooden desk leaned slightly forward in front of a lonely flag with forty-eight stars. At the opposite end of the room, a long white closet with sliding doors hid some ancient secret or crime. A bearded man, looking like an exile from Woodstock's rock festival, sat on a plastic chair and used a pointer to direct the students to repeat the smeared words on the board. When Sinclair entered, they all stopped repeating the words and stared at him, while ignoring Ms. Golden.

"This is your new teacher!" she announced proudly.

"The flag is out-of-date," Sinclair commented. She looked at it and grunted.

The substitute became visibly irritated, and he stood up, revealing his faded jeans and paisley shirt. "I have been assigned for the day," he protested.

"You can come to my office," Ms. Golden assured him without taking her eyes off the students. "Your new teacher's name is Mr. Sinclair."

She proceeded to write Sinclair's name. The screeching sound of the chalk echoed painfully as it reverberated throughout the room. Clapping her hands, Ms. Golden removed some of the sticky dust that would one day serve as a patina on an archeological find.

"Seen," a young Mexican girl, wearing a green dress, pronounced. "Claaar. ¡Hola! Señor."

"I don't speak Spanish," Sinclair immediately protested to Ms. Golden. He pointed out the Asian students. "And the other language or languages they speak."

"Much better if you don't," she dismissed his objection, "otherwise they won't learn English."

She smiled and reassured the young girl with a kind touch on her arm. The girl smiled nervously back at Ms. Golden.

"Let's go," she ordered the substitute.

"Les go, amigo," one of the Mexican boys repeated, trying to imitate her gusto. Ms. Golden giggled.

"Ciao, dude," the substitute waved to Sinclair and the students.

"Goo-," the students said almost in unison, "Bye, Meeser." They waved back at the substitute whose name they had never learned.

Ms. Golden gave Sinclair a reassuring smile. "See you later," she reminded him about the lesson plans. Without further ceremony, she followed the substitute out of the room. Sinclair could hear them rustle against the chain link fence as they walked alongside the agriculture area.

"OK," Sinclair said, feeling lost since he had nothing to teach. The students patiently watched him as he examined the board. Various vocabulary words, identifying objects in the room, had been written on the chalk-caked blackboard. The students, holding their pens in hand, were prepared to write more vocabulary words in their notebooks.

"OK . . ." Sinclair stalled, looking for some activity to fill the remaining half hour of the class. A couple of the students began to shift in their seats, and the young girl who had greeted him earlier gazed out the window on the farm area.

"Let's go," Sinclair shouted and walked towards the door, waving the five students towards him. "Come. Bring your notebooks." He gestured for them to hold the notebooks and pens in hand.

They looked skeptically at him and at each other. The girl took the initiative and followed Sinclair who stepped out onto the stoop. In a few seconds, the other students followed, and they all soon stood at the bottom of the stoop. Sinclair led them alongside the chain-link fence as the metal rattled and squeaked from they bodies rubbing against it. They passed the last bungalow and turned right, stepping into the agriculture area—the Ag field.

Two male students, wearing long rubber boots and holding buckets of meal for the animals, stood in front of the entrance to a small shack. They looked fatigued and bored.

"I teach ESL over there," Sinclair explained. "Where's your teacher?"

"He comes in at ten," one boy explained.

"Can I take these kids on a tour?" Sinclair asked. The two students looked at one another and shrugged.

"Yeah," one of them spoke. "I got to feed the animals before the next class."

"Thanks," Sinclair said, without exchanging another word. He walked past the shack and into the agriculture area. Confused, the

ESL students followed him until he stopped inside the fenced area. Several chickens and ducks greeted the visitors, expecting to be fed. The Ag field students arrived and began to spread the meal. Soon, more birds appeared.

"Chicken," Sinclair pointed to the animals.

One of his students spoke first. "Pollo," he said.

"Chicken," Sinclair repeated.

He took one boy's pen and wrote the word in his notebook. Sinclair shared the word with the other students. The Asian students remained quiet but dutifully followed Sinclair's instructions. They unconsciously compared their notes.

"Chicken," Sinclair repeated. All the students wrote the word, "chicken," in their notebooks and made an effort to pronounce the word. Sinclair continued to next bird.

"Duck," he named the bird. Twenty minutes passed quickly as Sinclair and the students identified and wrote the names of the animals in their notebooks. The young girl drew pictures of the animals and even sketched an impromptu portrait of Sinclair. He looked at his portrait and proudly held it up for the others to see. Later, she would become a famous local artist.

"This is good," he told her. She understood his congratulatory tone and smiled appreciatively.

All of a sudden, one student cried out, just as the bell rang for the next period. "¡Mierda!" the boy screamed and began to wipe the sole of his shoe on the chain-link fence. They had been standing near the cow, and the boy accidentally stepped into a cow pie.

"Shit!" Sinclair said in English. They all phonetically wrote the word down in their notebooks. The boy, who had stepped into the cow pie, furiously tried to clean off the remaining clod stuck between the sole and heel of his shoe.

"¡Mierda!" he complained aloud. "Sheeeett!"

"You're right, sheeett!" Sinclair said.

February Intermission

Sanchez sat home alone, almost relishing his victory. He asked the question that had been weighing on his mind, and the lecture erased any doubts. He had made up his mind. He was sure. He wanted to stay a teacher. But it was going to be easier said than done. On

Friday, Nick had listened to Sanchez as he recapped the lecture and then had stormed out without waiting to hear his decision.

Once again Nick had abandoned their home—this time for good. Sanchez needed to prepare to greet his students the next day. Tonight he would balance himself against the triumph of his classroom victory, the decision he had finally reached, and the loss of a husband.

Smith took his lunch break in his small storage room where he kept his samovar. Waiting for the tea water to boil, he sat and composed a handwritten note to his love interest, Helen, inviting her to the opera. In the background, Leoncavallo's aria, *Vesti la Giubba*, played melodically and sadly, diffusing an aura of peace and comfort. Holding the tickets in his hand, Smith dreamed of Helen, as he savored Puccini and the aria's every note, nuance, and words with adulation and aesthetic wonder. Deep down, Smith knew she was the woman who would complement his journey into a new life, career, and love. Later, he decided that he would place the tickets and the letter in her purse to surprise her.

The water began to boil and to steam, and Smith took a break to pour himself some tea in his favorite French china demitasse.

"You still drinking that stuff?" an undesirable voice barked from the edge of the doorway.

Smith, to his consternation, saw Rubio holding a dirty plunger. "There's a spill in the upstairs women's bathroom," Rubio grumbled and stuck the dripping plunger into his room. "It's the one in the faculty room."

Smith, disbelieving, watched fecal-infested water drip onto the cleanly polished tiles of his storeroom. "What about the environmental engineer?" Smith suggested, feeling sick, as he raised his cup to his lips.

He swallowed the bile that began to climb up his esophagus to supplant the taste of his tea. The sight of the plunger washed away the aesthetic feelings he had enjoyed a few moments before.

The toilet had backed up twice in one week.

"Screw that bastard!" Rubio dismissed his suggestion. "You got to fix it."

"What?" Smith objected sternly, smelling the offal in the water. "I'm on lunch."

Rubio thought about his words and then dropped the plunger at the doorway. "After," he accepted Smith's explanation.

Looking at the samovar, Rubio took—without asking permission—another demitasse nearby and poured himself a cup of tea. Smith began to seethe.

"You want sugar?" he croaked.

"No," Rubio declined and finished the tea in one gulp. "Good. I'm sorry, but this machine can't be here. I told you about it."

"Why not?" Smith demanded to know, nearly dropping his empty cup in his lap.

"They'll have an inspection next month," Rubio tried to sound apologetic. "After they go, you can bring it back."

He forced a congenial smile and turned around. Smith saw a wet patch of water seep from the plunger and spread in his general direction.

"Why can't Lapworth fix it?" Smith wanted to know. "He does shit."

"He's full of shit, too," Rubio agreed, facing Smith as he returned the cup. "Fix it soon." Rubio saluted and left.

When he had disappeared, Smith heard from his iPod player, Pavarotti's Pagliaccio laugh and cry. The putrid puddle approached his feet like a rising tide.

"No," Smith spoke to himself. "I won't be a clown." The infested water finally reached his shoes, and he belched while trying to splash it away from his chair. Smith seized the plunger and hurled it into the hallway. Smith's letter and tickets fell into the effluent puddle.

Chapter 16

March 2034
Sinclair

"Three . . . you still waiting?"
—Fernando Smith (The Janitor)

Sinclair sat in Stile's office with Asma and Middy, the First Priority Club president, who had a demure personality and usually spoke in a soft and measured tone—so unlike Asma. The date for their debate had been scheduled already. Stile wished to keep the debate civil since the topic invited controversy: whether God was real or not.

"Middy," Stile addressed her kindly. "Where's your club sponsor? Ms. Frank?"

"She had an emergency," Middy answered factually.

"She didn't call me," Stile complained in a slightly condescending tone. "What kind of an emergency?"

"I don't know," she admitted impatiently, maintaining a controlled tone. Middy expressed just a hint of exasperation.

Asma looked at Sinclair, who sat beside her, and smiled at Stile who ignored her congenial comportment.

"So," Stile spoke directly to Sinclair, "I'll tell you what I wanted to tell Ms. Frank."

Sinclair remained silent, knowing fully the purpose of the meeting and the issue that annoyed Stile and other conservatives on the staff. "I do not want a screaming match," Stile warned. "You know how I feel . . . no insults or harangue of any kind will be tolerated! I also have to warn you that . . . "

"We don't expect any," Middy interrupted him. "So we have a plan. Sorry."

Startled at first, Stile slowly expressed interest in her words, "Go ahead," he invited her to explain.

"Well," Middy fudged a bit and looked as Asma." We both put together something that can work better than a debate."

"It's educational," Asma inserted energetically.

Stile studied them both and looked at Sinclair who shrugged. "They put it together," he said, begging off any responsibility. In reality, Sinclair knew little about the club presidents' plans for the debate.

"OK," Asma said. She and Middy had known that Stile would be more tolerant if Middy had presented the plan. But she took the opportunity now to further explicate the plan. "OK?" she asked.

Stile expressed gravitas, but he extended his hand as a sign of indulgence. Middy tried to make eye contact with Asma, who was focusing exclusively on Stile.

"We think the question of God's existence is one of the big questions in life," she began in a rapid voice. "So Middy and I decided that a regular debate had too many drawbacks and could possibly lead to some regrettable issues."

"Yes," Stile concurred, relaxing his posture. "I don't want a yelling free-for-all. This is why I had my doubts about pursuing a debate from the very beginning."

"That's what we thought," Middy responded and waited. Stile expressed encouragement. Sinclair made eye contact with both girls in a silent plea for them to speed up.

"The normal debate takes too much time," Asma continued truthfully. "Three hours that we don't have. And we're meeting in a club setting after school, so it's not a formal environment. So we took a novel approach to the subject about God. The usual questions are too boring."

"Right," Middy agreeably concurred and sat up. She extracted a sheet of paper from a folder and handed it to Asma, along with copies for Stile and Sinclair.

"Ms. Frank has the original," Middy pointed out. Stile studied the paper. Sinclair glanced at Asma as he tried to ascertain the source.

"As you can read," Middy illuminated. "We composed twenty statements for discussion."

"Not debate," Asma clarified.

Stile looked up, trying to comprehend their proposal.

"Using old debate styles, I would say, *I assert the affirmative*," Middy spoke in a mocking tone, *"that God exists."*

"Then," Asma continued with her role-playing. "I would respond with, *I assert the negative that God doesn't exist."*

"I don't understand, ladies?" Stile interrupted them. "Isn't this a debate?"

"Not a formal one," Middy emphasized again.

"Give us some more details," Sinclair encouraged, noticing that Stile had reached a mental impasse.

"OK," Asma accepted the baton. "Our twenty statements reduce the time that is needed and the other problems with long, boring debates."

"But the differences are still addressed and discussed," Middy cleared up. "We won't use rebuttals and cross-examinations."

"Please," Stile stopped them. "Give me an example."

Sinclair shot a warning look at Asma who quickly dominated the dialogue.

"We start off with an opening statement of only six hundred words," Asma explained, lowering her voice and speaking ponderously. "Rebuttals are short, like one hundred to two hundred words. And the closing statement is short. Less than 100 words."

Stile expressed some curiosity.

"We touch on the debate topic for twenty minutes only," Middy persisted cheerfully. "And we got rid of the old traditional topics. Now we have new ideas without a timekeeper. Go ahead."

"What?" Stile asked in confusion.

"Choose a statement," Asma invited him to participate in a mock practice.

"OK," Stile agreed and scanned the statement. *"If there is no God, then life has no meaning."*

"That's mine," Middy volunteered happily. "I have all the even numbers. Those are the Christian statements."

"And I have the odd numbers," Asma added curtly. "The non-religious statements."

Stile read the statements and snarled when he read the non-religious ones. Sinclair read them, too, and appeared to be satisfied with the direction of the statements.

"These seem to be fair," Sinclair declared to Stile. "Everything is in balance. I like this one: *The Biblical God does not care much about animals.*"

"I like animals," Middy admitted, expressing an aversion to the idea of animal cruelty.

"We all do," Stile assured her.

"We have these statements," Asma returned to the agenda. "And we have a discussion. It's more practical and constructive."

"I think so," Middy agreed.

Stile looked at Middy and then at Asma before turning to face Sinclair. "What do you think, Mr. Sinclair?" Stile asked him.

"Yes. I think . . ." Sinclair began to speak.

Pierce entered the room and interrupted the meeting. "Good," he said without apologizing for the interruption. His smile was linear and cold. Uneasiness permeated the room; Pierce always projected a feeling of disquiet. "The debate?" Pierce clarified the reason for the meeting.

"Yes," Stile answered, adopting an official tone. "We were talking about the protocols of the debate."

"Good," Pierce repeated. "But I'm sorry."

"What?" Asma instantly objected, showing her immediate displeasure. "We can't have it?"

Pierce slightly shuddered at her outburst. Sinclair shot her a warning glance. Ironically, Stile appeared displeased that the debate could be canceled.

"You can," Pierce countered, suppressing his annoyance. "But not on campus."

Coyly, Middy raised her hand. "Why?" she simply asked.

"Well," Pierce appeared to be struggling to find the correct words, "it's the budget."

"Excuse me?" Stile suddenly became interested and irritated. "The school budget?"

"Downtown," Pierce responded and cleared his throat. "It's out of my hands. The district is forcing me to return club funds. I have to borrow from the discretionary fund."

"My committees and activities?" Stile became very agitated.

"Sorry," Pierce offered his bureaucratic, disarming smile to Stile. "We have to adhere to the rules. You have to make adjustments, Mr. Stile. I'll call a meeting tomorrow with club sponsors and everyone involved. But we're still here for the students, and we must continue to carry on. You're still employed for the year. I don't know about your assignment next year. I hope the district funds the activities department. I'll lobby for it. I promise. Thank you." He quickly slipped out of the room.

"With a stroke of the pen," Stile commented, contemplating the fact that his job had been eviscerated, "nothing."

Sinclair looked at him and instinctively compared Stile's dilemma with his own career and the challenges Smith faced.

"We won't put up with it!" Asma angrily avowed.

She stood up and held her arm out in defiance, like Delacroix's Lady Liberty leading the French people against the French aristocracy.

"I don't think we have a choice," Middy disagreed and stood up. "They can cancel it if they want to."

"They can," Asma agreed nominally. "But we won't put up with it."

Ignoring Middy and Sinclair, she stormed out, leaving confusion in her wake.

"Full of Sturm und Drang," Stile commented.

"Goethe would approve," Sinclair replied. "As long as she doesn't end like Faust or Werther."

"Werther?" Stile repeated, lost in his thoughts. "I remember reading the novel in college. Sad story." They remained silent for an awkward moment until Stile spoke again.

"Well," he sadly concluded. "Good effort, Middy." Stile could not think about saying anything else.

Sinclair was lost for words, too. Finally, he responded, breaking the awkward silence, "Well. Let's see how we can make this into a positive later."

Stile nodded and looked dejectedly down at his notes. "I'm finished. No job here for sure."

Despite their differences, Sinclair genuinely felt sorry for him. "Tomorrow, Mr. Stile?" calling his attention as he tried to dismiss himself from the room.

"Yes," Stile answered, reluctant to speak about the topic at length. "Tomorrow."

Sinclair nodded approvingly and stepped out of the office with Middy. When they were outside, Middy turned to face him. "What's going to happen?' she asked, bewildered.

"Don't know," he admitted, looking back at Stile's office. "Let see what happens within the next week. Your sponsor should communicate with you about any changes."

Middy accepted his description of the situation and pensively walked away. "Bye, Mr. Sinclair, and thanks," she murmured.

"Bye," he automatically answered. Sinclair would have to wait until tomorrow, next week, and maybe next school year. But waiting was not an option in his career or life. He took another look at Stile's office and wondered if Stile could wait, too. He then left to search for Asma.

It would be a futile endeavor. She was on a mission.

Chapter 17

March 2034
Sanchez

One evening there was a knock on the door, and, when Sanchez got up from correcting schoolwork, he was surprised to see Nick standing there. They talked and talked. After a few days, they decided to visit the place where their relationship had begun—the place where they had fallen in love.

It would turn out to be a bad decision for both of them.

Nick and Sanchez traveled to their favorite seafood restaurant on the wharf in Santa Barbara. In the early spring, the gray sea gave way to the burgeoning blue-green waters that shone brilliantly under a sinking California sun. Above the pier, a seagull squawked triumphantly, carrying a squirming sardine, which soon became a matter of fierce dispute with the other seagulls.

Years earlier, the restaurant had burned down, but when it was rebuilt, the couple had continued their patronage with almost fanatical loyalty. Inside, they spoke cordially and avoided any reference to their careers. In due time, Sanchez came to believe that Nick had resigned himself to his decision to be a teacher. However, for a short while, Nick appeared distracted and aloof about their day-to-day activities. Then it happened. Nick excused himself to go to the restroom, and absentmindedly left behind his iPhone. While he was away, the phone vibrated, and Sanchez saw the message.

Nick returned to an empty table.

He looked for Sanchez until a waiter told him that he saw him storm out. He paid the waiter in cash and rushed out of the restaurant to find Sanchez sitting on an antique brass cannon that overlooked the picturesque bay.

Nick had been unfaithful. When Sanchez confronted him about it, the worst possible scenario played out.

"Are you?" Sanchez asked, feeling as if his heart had imploded. Nick had been the love of his life. He could not imagine having any other person in his life. With or without his teaching career, Nick was a part of his existence.

"Come on!" Sanchez demanded. "You got to tell me."

Nick remained stoically inert.

"Nick!" Sanchez pleaded.

"I did it for you," he barely croaked.

Sanchez, bewildered, looked at him and shook his head.

"You did what?" . . . For me?" Sanchez repeated hatefully. "What kind of shit is that? For me?"

"You," Nick tried to continue, but he fell silent.

"Me?" Sanchez suddenly read his mind. "You got the law school acceptance for me with your connection. That was what it was all about?"

Sanchez turned around and stared at the sea, as he tried to repress his tears and anger.

"I should've known," Sanchez sadly admitted.

Nick touched his arm, and Sanchez twisted away, almost swiping at it.

"Go fuck off, Nick," he told him agonizingly. "And go fuck your connection, too."

Nick stared at his partner and then decided to walk off. Sanchez had the car keys, and he did not care where Nick walked off as the setting sun tinged the bright blue sky with streaks of red and orange.

The hunting seagull returned without the sardine and made a feeble dive into the bay waters, but failed to retrieve more fish. Sanchez watched the bird make several attempts until another seagull succeeded and the original seagull pursued it with reverse revenge.

Sanchez turned his face towards the parking lot to look for his car. It sat parked near an ice cream shop that served a few brave customers who ignored the dipping evening temperatures. Spring had arrived, but the mild California winter continued to hold court, receiving assistance from the frigid Alaskan currents.

Sanchez again looked in the direction of his car. Nick was not there.

"Asshole," Sanchez cursed and regretted his words. "He never listened."

Deep down, Sanchez wished Nick would return, and he knew he could—maybe—forgive him. He wanted to forgive him. So, he futilely waited.

The deep orange sun set, and in the twilight the Pacific Ocean rolled eternally—unaware of the life forms it involuntarily shouldered across the eons of time as its waves lapped the fragile coastline that incrementally moved away from the North American plate.

Sanchez sat and waited until the sun had set, and the crescent moon had risen on the western horizon, revealing a glassy, abandoned seascape. From his solitary perch on the antique cannon, he watched the moon's reflection dance on the undulating seawater amid the darkness of the night.

March Intermission

Sinclair spent another weekend working on his motorbike as he tried to stem a leak in the fuel line. The bike was ready to go, but he tried two different defective lines that the manufacturer had sent. Few fuel lines for motorbikes were manufactured during an era of lithium-powered and fuel-cell vehicles. Although his progress on the bike was stalled, his health had improved. The rehabilitation shots had lessened his fatigue, and his strong memory had returned. The physical improvements were easy to measure, but the personal challenges annoyed him.

The proverbial clock was ticking. He needed to decide whether to revise or alter the status of his sabbatical. Yet his decision was still at an impasse. He needed to find one important element: What was important to him?

"To continue in life," Sinclair thought, "with a purpose."

On a personal level, Rachel officially made it known that their relationship was at an end. A Japanese attorney sent the divorce papers through international legal channels. Fortunately, Sinclair could stay at his home once Rachel returned in the summer. Sooner or later he would have to leave.

"Delaying the inevitable," he embraced the small comfort of meager time.

His improving health had not provided Sinclair with the advantage of youth—boundless carefree time. He now had too much to care for and too few options. At least, he had a few months until Rachel returned and he began his new career training—if that is what he ultimately decided.

"Do I really have more time?" he wondered. Currently, Sinclair was living on borrowed time until a bureaucratic behemoth dictated the terms of his life, career, and time.

But he held an ace in his hands. Something no one could know. He wondered if he were still young enough to pursue the option. Once he was sure—when Sophie had entered his life long ago. Something in his past held the key to a decision. His improving memories hinted that an answer danced at the edge of his conscious. He believed it was within reach.

He felt it! He also perceived that he was, perhaps, deceiving himself for the sake of gaining more time. "Time to do what?" he pondered.

Opera is an art form that people either love or hate. Helen hated it! Smith worshipped opera, and he could not fathom anyone else disliking it. "Hey, baby," Smith spoke to Helen after the opera *Tosca* ended and the final bows ceased with the curtain fall. "Wasn't that *magnífico*?" Smith asked, as he applauded enthusiastically at the end.

Helen was silent. During the intermission, Smith did all the talking, and Helen listened. She visited the restroom, accepted a drink, and simply listened, offering a reserved smile to her host. Sometimes, she said, "Sí."

Smith ignored the signs of the impending tragedy. He was dressed in his best suit, recently purchased. Admiring Helen's long, black sequined gown, he lusted after her like the malevolent character, Scarpia, in the opera. Helen's dress hid the treasure of his dreams. Her love would be his salvation. She was his religion—after opera, of course.

"The diva had an angelic voice, no?" Smith demanded desperately, as he struggled to resist appraising her body.

"Sí," Helen repeated all evening but refrained from offering any personal insights or opinions. They strolled out of the crowded Dorothy Chandler Pavilion in downtown Los Angeles. The air was cool, and Helen immediately put on, with Smith's gentlemanly assistance, her cashmere cardigan. Smith had bought it for her from his paltry savings. In fact, Smith paid for everything that evening.

Taking a generous tip from Smith, the college-age valet promptly delivered his expensive rental car. Surrounding the couple were upper-class opera fans and sponsors awaited the delivery of their own Cadillacs, Jaguars, and Mercedes-Benzes. Smith and Helen blended into the crowd so well that they exchanged banal pleasantries and comments with some of them. Delighted at the turn of events, Smith had become a temporary member of the haut monde.

"Sir," the valet called, pointing to Smith's car. He opened the passenger door of the rental BMW and escorted Helen to her seat before closing the door. He then sprinted to the driver's side to hand the keys to Smith, who reluctantly, paid the valet another tip. It was expected.

"Thank you," the young man snatched the tip and dashed to another highborn customer.

Smith growled under his breath as he began to calculate the cost of the evening. Casting his eye on Helen, he quickly forgot his resentment and the loss of a significant portion of his precious savings.

"So," Smith insisted when he began to drive away. "What do you think?"

Helen only smiled.

He sped away from the Pavilion and accelerated the BMW across Grand Avenue to enter the Hollywood Freeway entrance going north. Once they were on the dilapidated freeway, she spoke.

"I," Helen confessed carefully "didn't like it much."

Confounded, Smith groaned.

"It was beautiful," she added defensively. "But it was silly."

"Silly?" Smith questioned, shocked.

"Yes," Helen continued confidently. "Why didn't she just fuck the policeman? Then everything would have been OK. He said he would save her lover. She would have had what she wanted. The boyfriend wouldn't have been dead either."

Her explanation left Smith speechless.

"No real woman would let that happen," Helen concluded. "Stupid."

Smith fumed.

"But the music was beautiful," she added with aplomb.

Smith's heart pounded furiously. He had not expected Helen to offer such a callous perspective about great art and true love.

"It's about the ultimate love and her sacrifice," Smith stumbled for an argument.

"Stupid woman," Helen retorted. "She lost everything. All she would have lost was her virginity. Big deal."

Smith's mind reeled with arguments, counterarguments, and angry thoughts. No one argument escaped his lips as he drove the BMW to Helen's home. He was flummoxed. But he held out hope that the evening would not be a complete loss. In less than thirty minutes, Smith arrived at Helen's condominium.

"Thank you," Helen said, as she gestured for Smith to park outside her complex. "I'm tired. The music was wonderful. Really. Thank you for everything. Thank you for the beautiful clothes and sweater. Maybe something different next time? No?"

She leaned over to kiss Smith's cheek and swiftly opened her door.

"Wait," he feebly called out. "I paid for . . ."

"Goodnight," she responded before slamming the door shut.

He incredulously watched her leave.

"I like the car," she shouted without turning around.

"Buenas noches," Smith muttered. "Good night."

He watched, incredulous, as she navigated the walkway on spike heels with hurried steps. At her door, she rapidly punched in the codes for the door lock and disarmed the alarm. Swiftly, she slipped into her condo and disappeared.

"Puta!" he cursed. "Bitch!" The weight of the evening's debt became an encroaching and frightful reality. He was broke and broken.

Chapter 18

April 2034
Sanchez

"Oh . . . when I tell you . . . you won't like it."
—Fernando Smith (The Janitor)

The news came hard.

The avarice of the bureaucratic machine was deadly. Every club received the announcement for the emergency meeting. Waiting for Pierce and the club principals to arrive, Sinclair and Asma assembled with the school's staff in the media center. Sanchez remained behind to supervise the lab.

The media pavilion had once been state-of-the-art when the school first opened. Glass block walls created an aerial ambiance that illuminated every corner and angle of the room, and a team of four librarians and three technicians guided inquisitive and ignorant students through mazes of index card catalogues and rows of books. As decades passed, however, neglect replaced innovation. Dysfunctional Smart Boards and archaic computers lined the walls, far from the deactivated Ethernet plugs under rundown kiosks. These had given way to portable tablets and smartphones that logged into the Wi-Fi infrastructure. The old desktops gave way to portable clouds, and the librarians evaporated into virtual memories. They, along with the archaic paper tombs of knowledge, disappeared slowly, but eventually it was permanent.

When Pierce called for the emergency meeting, Asma, as usual, received the news before Sinclair.

When they arrived, no one stood at the front desk to greet them. The media pavilion was staffed by only one media technician, who never appeared from her closet refuge of electronic junk. She had once been a librarian but had to change her job title to save her job. Now, like Sinclair, she faced the unknown future of rehabilitation. Hearing the din of people entering the center, she appeared with consternation and bewilderment. Pierce had failed to inform her of the meeting.

"Hi, Ms. Paula," hailed Sinclair. She was tall, dark, and svelte, with an athletic figure that precluded the need for rehabilitation. "How's it going?" Sinclair added automatically with a friendly smile.

She expressed a look of bafflement.

"Emergency meeting," Sinclair notified her. Ms. Paula accepted the revelation with little interest. Lately, they hardly spoke to each other, yet silently relished long lost conversations. Today was different.

"Hi, Ms. Paula," Asma saluted her and then instinctively began to search for her friends and acquaintances. "I'll save you a seat," she told Sinclair as she left without waiting for a reply. Sinclair did not speak until she was a safe distance away. Ms. Paula wanted to speak privately to him.

"Hi," Laura's voice interrupted Sinclair, just as he started to speak to Ms. Paula.

"Hey," he uncomfortably acknowledged her.

Since his meeting with the attorney, Laura had kept her distance. She stared at him for a moment now. "We still have to talk," Laura mentioned to Sinclair.

"Not until I talk to him first," Ms. Paula joked.

Laura tried to grasp her meaning. "Good," she understood and laughed. "Later, Mark." She walked away, and Sinclair waited for her to move out of earshot.

"OK," Sinclair agreed uneasily.

The experience with the attorney and his personal entanglements caused him to feel suddenly awkward.

"Come with me," Ms. Paula invited him. "This will be interesting."

Sinclair gladly followed her through a labyrinth of old VCR players, projectors, overhead machines and derelict copiers. In one corner, stacks of moldy boxes lay open.

"Look inside," she invited Sinclair. He instinctively held his breath and winced as he looked inside.

"What?" he asked. "Coasters?"

"No," she impatiently answered.

Lightly pushing him aside, she reached into the box and extracted a square blue-colored plastic disk. "Floppies," she declared. "Can you believe it?"

"As I said," Sinclair repeated, "what?"

"Hoarded from the late 1990s," Ms. Paula spoke scornfully. "These administrators hoarded disks, pens, pencils, composition notebooks, folders . . ." She then pointed to more boxes in the far corner.

"Junk for the bins," Ms. Paula decided on their destination. "But I can't without authorization. . . . It's still catalogued!" She sadly passed her hand over the boxes and closed the covers. "What a shame."

"I like pencils," Sinclair tried to humor her.

She scornfully glared at him, and he backed off. "I'm not joking," he assured her. "I do like pencils."

Ignoring him, she secured the boxes. "I do, too," she admitted. "Ridiculous!"

"Yes," Sinclair agreed lamentably.

"Is this what we will become, too?" she inquired reflectively. Sinclair wanted to answer, but he could only shake his head. "I miss our heart-to-heart talks," she admitted.

"Yeah, . . . life complicates everything."

"No, . . . we do. I'm showing this to you because I don't want us to become refuse in a catalogue."

Sinclair grasped her allusion and wished to address it. They both had something important to say to one another during this crisis in their lives.

In the distance, they heard Pierce's voice. "Got to go," Sinclair excused himself. "See ya," he told her as he hurried back to the main hall. He stumbled on some wires and knocked over an overhead on his way out. When he entered the room, Pierce and the club members stared in his direction. A few students conversed and giggled.

"Please join us," Pierce gravely invited Sinclair.

He meekly walked over to a wooden chair that Asma had reserved for him. She refused to make eye contact when he sat down, so he lightly leaned into her. Next to her sat Middy who smiled at Sinclair.

"Thanks," he whispered. Asma grimaced and remained silent.

"Well," Pierce began again. The media pavilion remained eerily silent. "The activities department," Pierce cleared his throat. "The . . . activities department is suspended this school year."

An uproar of voices erupted into a confusing melee of debate and accusations.

Pierce waited several moments to allow the initial reactions to subside. He then raised his hands, signaling them to be silent. Slowly, the clamor diminished, and an anxious reserve replaced the crowd's loud outburst.

"Is it the funding?" the fashion club sponsor questioned loudly.

"No," Pierce rejected the accusation. "It was an issue, but it is not the primary issue now." He stared with glassy eyes at the audience.

"Mr. Stile," Pierce spoke with deliberate emphasis, " . . . he's passed on. The district sadly . . . and tragically informed me that he is dead."

"What?" an unidentified voice bawled. The boisterous hubbub began again, but this time cries and sobs could be heard. Shocked, the club members soon lowered their voices, so they could hear the details.

"What happened?" another voice demanded to know. Pierce spoke directly into the wireless microphone he held in his hand. "He had a stroke this morning," he sadly revealed. "We do not know the details. When I have information about the funeral arrangements, I'll let you know. The family asks that you respect their privacy at this moment. Thank you. That's all I have now."

"What about our fund drives," another club sponsor shouted. "Some of us have collections in process."

Pierce had prepared to leave but addressed the concern. His heart was not into speaking.

"Please return all money to the treasurer," Pierce firmly instructed them. "I will contact our benefactors and explain the situation. Thank you again."

This time Pierce did not wait for questions and stepped out of the media pavilion, leaving his microphone with Ms. Paula at the desk. Sinclair remained sitting in a state of amazement. He did not personally like Stile, but he would never have wished for his death.

"I'm not going to take this," Asma told Sinclair with bravado.

"It's over," Sinclair reminded her. "They pulled the funding. Stile's death just puts a nail into it all. No pun intended."

"But the system killed him," Asma pounced on his words. "They took his love away. His career. A lot of people didn't like him, but he was a person that made a contribution."

Sinclair had no answer for her because he knew she was right. The termination of the funding ended the activities office's ability to function and made Stile an obsolete employee.

"I know we can't fight them," Asma avowed, "but I will try to do something. The public has to know."

"Right," Sinclair responded in a noncommittal tone. "You go try. Good luck."

Asma ignored his sarcastic response and, with Middy, joined some students who congregated behind the podium where Pierce had spoken. Asma and Middy quickly took control of the situation and began to formulate an impromptu game plan with some club presidents.

"Well, at least he didn't have to decide anything," Laura commented to Sinclair.

He swiftly turned around and saw her smirking as she stood above him.

"They left him few options anyway," Laura added. "He was lucky."

Sinclair stood up and faced her. "You know," Sinclair spoke cryptically, "we seem to have bizarre conversations during critical events."

Laura took a quick and nervous peek around the room. Everyone had gathered in small pockets to gossip about Stile's death. She and Sinclair were alone.

"My friend," Laura said seriously, "tells me that you have to decide soon. Really soon."

"I have a few months," Sinclair reminded her. "Tell him thank you."

"OK," Laura accepted the response. "I'm telling you to hurry up. They want an answer by the end of the semester, or you . . ."

"Won't have a choice," Sinclair filled in the blank. "I get it. But I won't let the same thing happen to me like it did to Stile. I won't let the system kill me. Don't worry."

Laura made another careful sweep with her eyes.

"This is serious," she berated him. "We . . . I . . . am putting my career . . . my life on the line."

"Yes," Sinclair said, affectionately touching her arm. "I appreciate it. But it's my decision. The only one I can make. In a way that makes me understand . . . truly understand what happened to Stile. Maybe he was lucky, and the choice was removed. You understand?"

They stared at each other, quietly sharing their anxiety about their choices at this critical juncture in their careers.

"Isn't this terrible?" Ms. Paula broke the spell.

They instinctively jumped when they heard her voice.

"Yes," Laura responded dreamily. "I feel sorry for his family."

"It's always bad for the family," Sinclair added remorsefully.

"Very bad," Ms. Paula concurred solemnly. "Very bad for us at the school. Especially for the children."

"Ah-ha," Sinclair murmured and made an effort to walk away. "Thank you, Laura," he excused himself. "Bye, ladies." He smiled feebly and walked through the media pavilion to the exit, while exchanging some words and condolences with the staff. At the exit door, he encountered Smith, holding a carpet cleaner.

"This is terrible," Smith commented sadly, keeping his eyes on the cleaner. He pensively rolled it back and forth. "People don't care for people. They do things that hurt, and the victims become desperate. They go crazy from the pain. It kills them cold!"

With a raised eyebrow and bulging, angry eyes, Smith shot a look of desperation at Sinclair. "This way," he spoke threateningly, "is not right. A price will be paid if they continue to walk on people. We are not carpet." He looked down and bitterly rolled the cleaner over the carpet. "We take care of things here better than people!" he affirmed emphatically, pointing his finger at the carpet. "Shit!"

Wretched, Smith patted Sinclair's shoulder and rolled the cleaner ahead. Sinclair wanted to ask him about Helen but decided that the moment was not right. Distressed, he observed Smith clean the carpet without making any eye contact or exchanging any words with the staff. Deciding that nothing could be done to lift Smith's spirits, Sinclair left the media center.

Outside, he caught a glimpse of Helen talking to Smith's supervisor, Rubio. Helen made eye contact with Sinclair, and then spoke to Rubio and walked away in the opposite direction. Rubio looked in Sinclair's direction and waved to him. Sinclair returned the salutation and watched Rubio disappear around the corner.

Sinclair noticed the hallway was empty and remembered that Sanchez was waiting to be relieved in the lab. He left thinking about Stile and the decisions he soon faced. Laura's reappearance did not ease the process.

He hoped he had better luck than Stile—staying alive just long enough.

Chapter 19

April 2034
Sanchez

After Sanchez heard the news, he spent some time talking to Sinclair. The students in the lab—through social media—had received the bad news before Sinclair arrived, and they had shared their reactions and comments with Sanchez who could not provide any details. Some of the students had muttered crude jokes.

"When did Stiles die?" Sanchez asked Sinclair.

"Not sure," Sinclair admitted. "Maybe in the early morning? I don't have the details."

"Bad," Sanchez contemplated. "How are the club members taking it?"

"Asma is on a rant," he revealed. "I won't stop her. What's the point?"

"It won't go anywhere," Sanchez said. He had resigned himself to the situation. "You know the news media is going to be all over this."

"Yeah," Sinclair agreed reluctantly. "Asma knows, too. It'll be a zoo here."

"Shit!" Sanchez gasped. "All those kids protesting and the media. What a mess!"

"I think so," Sinclair thought about the scenario. "But that's not my problem now."

"What?" Sanchez asked, surprised at Sinclair's stark apathy.

Sinclair recognized what he had said and tried to cover it up. "We'll take it one day at a time," he assured Sanchez. "Thanks for covering the class."

"Sure," he replied, glad for the opportunity to take a break. "I'm goin' to eat something."

"OK," Sinclair answered automatically. His mind was lost in his thoughts. "If you see Asma," he added seriously, "have her come by."

"Are you positive?" Sanchez questioned, visualizing Asma raving in front of a news camera.

"It can't get worse," he concluded.

For a moment Sanchez observed Sinclair—distracted and distant—and then he walked out of the lab. The students pretended to work on their assignments, but they were all involved in a perpetual conversation of rumors, gossip, and speculation. Stile's death would end the year on a sour note.

Once in the hallway, Sanchez noticed a light emanating from Smith's janitor closet. The odor of an exotic tea wafted through the corridor. Intrigued, Sanchez strolled towards the closet and began to hear the soft aria of an Italian opera. When he reached the closet, he discovered Smith passively sipping his tea from a bone china cup. His cleaning equipment stood ready behind him, and the Persian samovar brewed quietly next to his duster.

"Come in," Smith pleasantly invited him, while he turned down the music. "Mr. Sanchez?"

"Yes," Sanchez answered and stared at the samovar.

"You like it?" he queried proudly. When Sanchez nodded in the affirmative, he added, "me, too." Smith reached over and withdrew another bone china cup from a drawer. He handed it to Sanchez. "Would you like me to pour it?" he politely asked.

"Yes," Sanchez accepted, afraid of mishandling the antique work of art. "Earl Grey?"

"No," Smith poured him a hot cup of steaming tea. "Earl Grey is not popular in Persia."

He carefully handed it to Sanchez and opened his drawer again, extracting different colored packets. "Cream?" he asked. "Azuca?"

"A little sugar," Sanchez requested "Gracias."

He handed him a packet of sugar, and Sanchez gently poured it into his cup.

"De nada. I like the real stuff," Smith enjoyed watching Sanchez cherish the tea and sip it.

"Good," he complimented him. "Nothing online like this today."

"No," Smith concurred, taking a sip from his own cup. "This samovar is electric. But the best is coal-heated. I can't bring that here."

Sanchez surprisingly looked up at him.

"Really," he reacted, amazed. "Coal?"

Smith sipped his tea again and nodded, gesturing at the samovar.

"Can I look at it?" he could not resist the temptation.

"Let me show you," Smith cordially offered.

He put down his cup and disconnected the samovar from the outlet.

"It's interesting that you have an outlet," Sanchez commented.

"Yes," Smith spoke smugly. "The new machines all use the Tesla connection. I think all this radiation and radio signals are killing us."

Sanchez stepped to his side as Smith stood up with a little effort and moved towards the samovar.

"Look," Smith invited him. "You slide open the bottom. It allows you to close and open the chamber." Sanchez took a sip of tea and leaned over. "That's how you make it." Smith showed him and closed the samovar.

Sanchez made a careful examination of the exotic teapot. The lid had two brass knobs and a vent allowed the steam to escape. The samovar itself had two brass handles and a brass spout. Surrounding the samovar was a layer of silver displaying symmetrical designs and Persian script. Sanchez gently ran his fingers over the repetitive motif inlays.

"Beautiful," Smith commented, sitting down. "You like beauty, too. It comes from Borujerd. My other one comes from Russia. That is a real work of art, built with genuine artistic love." Sanchez smiled and continued to drink his tea.

"They call that German silver," Smith pointed out. "But it's not real silver. There's some nickel in it and copper too. But it looks silver. Like plata in Spanish. The decorations are typical for the religion. Muslims don't engrave pictures of people. It's idolatry to them."

Smith stopped speaking to reflect on his words and take another sip of tea. "We have too much idolatry in the West," he reflected, finishing his tea and standing up again.

Taking Sanchez's cup, he refilled it and then poured himself another cup of tea. Sanchez remained silent and enjoyed his tea. He did not want to fall into a debate with the cantankerous old man. "It's too bad," Smith spoke emphatically. "Too bad."

"What?" Sanchez was caught off guard.

"Señor Stile," Smith reminded him. "The man was brave. But not brave enough to survive the system."

Sanchez, confused, stared at Smith.

"Unlucky, too," Smith added, holding up a finger to the ceiling. "Any man can be both. Only a great man can be one. Either a fool or a hero."

Sanchez took another sip of hot tea as he tried to comprehend Smith's allusions. He was lost.

"You don't understand?" Smith asked, not expecting an answer. "The teacher needs a lesson on life." Smith smiled to himself and looked thoughtfully into his cup. Sanchez remained silent, as he tried to untangle his reasoning.

"Yes," Smith privately concluded. "This generation of gadgets has no commitment. To be great you must take the decision to its end."

"What do you mean?" Sanchez challenged softly, wishing to finish his tea and depart.

"Let me tell you," Smith answered didactically. "He died because they killed him. Everything was taken away. He had nothing. So he died. He was brave."

"I see," Sanchez lied, happy to consume the last sips. The tea left a bitter taste in his mouth.

"But he didn't do what he needed to do," Smith concluded abruptly. "He never had a chance to follow through on his . . . destiny. He lost his option to choose. A man ought to be able to choose!"

Smith's words further confused Sanchez. "What did he need to choose?" Sanchez was nearly afraid to ask.

Smith gaped at Sanchez and tilted his cup, almost spilling its contents. He angrily downed the remaining tea in his cup and stared inside it for a few seconds. Then he began to laugh aloud.

Nervous, Sanchez began to wonder if he had been speaking to a lunatic.

"It's OK, my friend," Smith consoled him. "I'm not laughing at you. It's your generation. It's everybody." He continued to laugh to himself and put his cup down. Extending his hand, he took Sanchez's cup and placed both cups in the corner washbasin. Then he straightened his shirt and fumbled with his cleaning cart as he prepared to go to work.

"What did he need to choose?" Sanchez insisted.

Smith chuckled a little and made direct eye contact with Sanchez. Stepping up to his face, Smith looked up and could feel Sanchez's breath brush his skin.

"Every man," Smith clarified deliberately, "must make that decision himself. Stile didn't have a chance to do it. But when the time comes, you must do it. I must do it. They must do it. Even women must do it. If you don't do it . . . well . . . what can I say?"

"Do what?" Sanchez pressed.

Smith lowered his head and maneuvered the cart into the doorway, while ignoring the question. "Thank you for coming," he said carelessly. "Maybe we can drink some tea together again in the future?"

"Bueno," Sanchez agreed politely but not sincerely.

The conversation bothered Sanchez. In truth, he had not wanted to speak. As he left the room, self-recriminations washed over him.

"Have a nice day," Smith wished him and pushed the cart through the doorway.

Sanchez followed him into the hallway. "Thank you," he told him, "for the exquisite tea." He peeked at the samovar before leaving.

"I know," Smith understood. "The Russian one is magnificent. I appreciate your good taste. Good luck, young man."

Smith began to whistle *Vesti la Giubba* and absentmindedly pushed his cart down the hallway. Sanchez smiled politely and walked past him to the exit. Soon leaving Smith behind, he glanced back and saw the janitor begin to wipe a stain off the wall. The class period ended, and students filed out of the labs. One male student approached Smith and had a brief but earnest exchange with him.

Sanchez curiously observed them and then exited the hallway. He sensed that Smith had more to say to him, to Sinclair, and to the world. He also had a feeling the news would not be good.

April Intermission

Smith's world began to collapse.

After work, he sat alone in his closet. He held a tepid cup of tea. In his free hand, he held his iPod that displayed an e-mail. The message contained a notice that his rehabilitation would be suspended until summer when he would enter a reorientation workshop. Rehabilitation would commence once he successfully completed the workshop requirement. The e-mail also referred Smith to a counselor for immediate psychological review. "Do not forget," it advised him. "Have a nice day!"

But the rehabilitation e-mail did not upset him as much as the video attachment from another email. His world slowly imploded, and he automatically dismissed the workshop as a superfluous event in his life.

"What's up Smith?" Kiki's voice broke the silence.

Smith stared at the iPod; he was not listening to his coworker's voice.

"Hey," she kicked his leg with her foot. "What are you doing? Something on the iPod?"

He painfully looked up from his iPod and glumly faced her as he unintentionally spilled the tea onto the tile floor. He could not speak.

"Smithy," she cried out, "you spilled the tea." She instinctively grabbed a washcloth and wiped the tea off his armrest and floor. As she cleaned up, he remained inert and self-absorbed. She gently took his cup out of his hand and placed it on the small table next to the samovar. "This thing is beautiful," she said, trying to get his attention.

"I sold the Russian one long ago," Smith admitted regretfully. "I lied to Sanchez."

Kiki then dropped the dirty cloth into a bin and washed her hands in the basin.

"Rubio is looking for you," Kiki reminded him. "You were supposed to be in the gym earlier."

"Rubio?" Smith muttered pensively. "I am finished. We all are finished. No más."

Smith dismissed Kiki with a wave of his hand and turned on his opera music.

She quietly listened to the music before speaking. "That will depress you more," she warned him.

"It's Leoncavallo," Smith challenged her. "What do you know?"

"I know you should go home," she instantly countered. "Take a sick day."

Smith ignored her recommendation.

"Rubio is looking for you," she reminded him again. "Tell him you're sick. . . . I'll tell him you're sick. You can go straight to the office and then home."

Smith continued to sit impassively in his chair. The old aria from *Pagliacci* began to hum loudly as he examined the photographs on his iPod.

"Is that Cinderella?" Kiki asked, amazed.

"Fuck that bitch!" Smith screamed and half-rose out of his chair. He fell back into it. "She's Helen and not Cinderella. I told you to get those fuckers out of there."

"What's on that thing?" Kiki probed inquisitively. Smith's belligerent reaction did not faze her.

Furiously looking at her, he slapped the iPod to his chest and pointed his finger at the door. "Go," he ordered her. "Leave me."

Fearful, Kiki left the room. "You better get help," she suggested as she stepped out.

"I have help," Smith retorted, "and life and death in my hands."

When she had gone, he slammed the closet door closed. "Crazy bitch!" he concluded irately.

Kiki left Smith to his personal misery and decided to clean her hands of the situation. Rubio could go to hell, too, including the bitch, Cinderella.

Kiki wrote him off—he was not worth the trouble.

———————————

The rehabilitation therapy led to a renewal of buried memories. Sinclair remembered his long weekend vacation with Sophie in San Francisco, back in 1984 before she left for Brazil. They drove up the Pacific Coast Highway through San Luis Obispo and Big Sur and stopped a few hours in Carmel and Monterey. The next day, they took a short boat ride to Alcatraz. Surrounding the island, the cold, crippling currents rippled towards the Golden Gate Bridge on their way out to the deep gray expanse of the Pacific Ocean. They joined a tour of the cells that once housed infamous prisoners such as the Bird Man and Al Capone. A section of the prison had been recently painted for a Clint Eastwood film about the only successful escape from rocky fortress. On the tour, the stark, bleak cells bore silent witness to the extreme deprivations suffered by most of the prisoners under the weight of life sentences.

"This must've been horrible," Sophie concluded.

"They committed horrible crimes," Sinclair reminded her. "For the time it must have been OK."

"I don't see," she skeptically rejected. "How?"

"For the ones who avoided the electric chair," he tried to explain. "As least for them they lived."

"What a bad life," she lamented.

Sinclair studied the bare concrete walls, cold steel bars, and generally dehumanizing facilities. Most cells only had a hole in the floor for a toilet.

"They made a choice that landed them here," Sinclair added reflectively. "Life sometimes gives you limited choices with serious consequences."

Sophie reexamined her surroundings.

"Who would choose to be here?" she speculated critically.

"No one," Sinclair agreed. "They made bad choices. They weren't careful or . . . wise, I guess."

He pulled her close and gave her a quick kiss. She tightly held his hand for the rest of the tour. They never commented on the prison again, while they finished the tour and returned to the boat. When they returned to Ghirardelli Square, a shipmate took their picture with Sinclair's Polaroid. Afterwards, they ate at Fisherman's Wharf with the other tourists who consumed sourdough bread bowls filled with clam chowder. Sinclair had forgotten about Alcatraz until the recent rejuvenation infusion allowed him to recall the experience in vibrant detail.

Abruptly, he had a small epiphany. He realized that he needed to be wise or end up in his own Alcatraz for the next eighty years.

Chapter 20

May 2034
Sanchez

"It's coming soon, my friend!"
—Fernando Smith (The Janitor)

Early Saturday morning, Sanchez arrived late with a rental truck. An LED advertisement on the truck boasted the company's commitment to the environment: *Fully Powered with Green Lithium*. A warm morning was becoming warmer when Sanchez drove up to Sinclair's driveway. Some of his friends had helped him load the truck, but they had left it to Sanchez and Sinclair to finish unloading it themselves. Despite Sinclair's invitation, Sanchez felt uncomfortable about moving into his mentor's house.

Circumstances had forced Sanchez's hand since Nick terminated the rental agreement at the beginning of the month. Even though Sanchez had postponed the inevitable, it was expected. With some muscle and sweat, both men unloaded the truck in two short hours. Fortunately, Sanchez possessed few items. He moved into an empty room that Sinclair's son had once used.

"Clean up," Sinclair suggested. "I'll make some lunch."

Sanchez suddenly became aware of his hunger and realized that he had been suppressing it all day. After cleaning up, he met Sinclair in the kitchen. His mentor served him a hoagie sandwich, salad, and some chips.

"Here's something that'll refresh you," Sinclair said, producing two open bottles of beer.

Sanchez gladly accepted the bottle and quickly drank down half of the brew.

"Thirsty," he declared, with his mouth watering for the delicious-looking hoagie.

"Eat," Sinclair invited him. "Don't be like Pavlov's poor dog."

Sanchez laughed and immediately devoured half his sandwich and finished the rest of the beer.

"I have more," Sinclair promised and retrieved another bottle of cold beer.

"Oh," Sanchez moaned gratefully. "I needed this bad."

"Go ahead," Sinclair encouraged him. "You're a growing boy." He continued chomping on his own hoagie and put it down only to quaff a large amount of his second beer.

"You're right," Sanchez agreed and burped. Sanchez laughed with a full mouth and chewed cheerfully. Sinclair joined him. They watched each other eat for several moments before speaking.

"Thanks again for rescuing me," Sanchez expressed his gratitude.

"I understand," Sinclair said empathetically. "I'll be in the same boat soon." He looked at Sanchez and nodded. "Both of us," he halfheartedly joked, "are orphans of unrequited love."

Sanchez snorted at the cryptic joke, since Sinclair faced a divorce and impending eviction once his wife returned and the judge ordered a settlement. Yet the future was too far away for both men, and they buried their anxious thoughts to turn to the present moment and enjoy it. Today, they had enough challenges.

"Looks like the rehabilitation stuff is helping you," Sanchez commented on Sinclair's stamina that morning.

Sinclair grinned and washed down a mouthful of food and beer. "Yeah," Sinclair confirmed. "It makes me feel less tired. That's what I noticed. I have more energy."

Sanchez thought quietly and took another bite. "Did you decide?" he pensively asked, still eating.

Almost choking, Sinclair took a quick swig of beer and pushed down the irritating food morsels. "Decide?" he questioned.

Sanchez wanted to respond but let Sinclair think through the question. "Oh," Sinclair understood. "I did . . . but later."

"Later?" Sanchez asked, stopping his chewing.

"When I'm ready," Sinclair assured him in a friendly manner. "You'll be one of the first to know. Promise."

He held up his two fingers in a Boy Scout salute. Sanchez agreeably nodded and accepted Sinclair's pledge.

"You were a Boy Scout?" Sanchez inquired skeptically.

"Many moons ago, Chief."

Sanchez snickered and continued to eat. "OK," he responded pleasantly, respecting Sinclair's privacy.

"You know," Sinclair began to wax philosophically. "Decisions can be tough. Even easy ones. You got to think carefully about the consequences."

Sanchez studied him and smiled.

"Are you getting mushy?" he gibed.

"No," Sinclair allayed his apprehension. "I'm serious." Sinclair's gravitas caught Sanchez's attention. "It's important," he continued. "I mean decisions are."

"OK," Sanchez encouraged him as he finished his lunch. "Go ahead."

Sinclair took another long drink from his bottle and paused to reflect on his next words. "It's really simple," he explained. "Decisions—the real ones—define us as persons. When we make our own decisions," he repeated, "they contribute to making us who we are. It's a definition of ourselves. And if it fails, that's OK, too. It's not the failing that matters; . . . it's the doing."

"The doing?" Sanchez asked.

"It is better to do something than nothing," Sinclair blurted out. "Most people sit around in life and wait for things to happen. I want to make it happen, and I can blame no one else for its failure. It's really disgusting when people go around and blame others for doing things they themselves should have done."

"So you made your decision?" Sanchez asked again.

"Yes," Sinclair declared proudly. "And it's wonderful, I hope. But that doesn't matter either."

Sanchez waited for details, but Sinclair gave him none. So he decided to change the subject. "The lunch was great," he complimented his host. "I'm going to get fat here."

Sinclair guffawed. "Maybe not, but we have to get the house in order for the lawyers, and you're going to help after the school session."

"OK," Sanchez promised and returned the Boy Scout salute. "At least before we're homeless."

They both laughed at the impending termination of their living arrangements.

"I see you have that motorbike in the garage," Sanchez referred to Sinclair's project.

"There's my next decision," Sinclair revealed to him. "To get it running before I am homeless. I'm going to need it to get around and find a new place."

They laughed together again. Without prompting, Sanchez stood up and began to clean up after himself. Sinclair tried to object, but he told him, "Please. It's my honor."

"OK," Sinclair agreed and wandered off to wash up and change clothes after the morning's move.

Sanchez cleaned up the mess and washed the dishes. When he finished, he put away the dishes and glasses, just as Sinclair returned. Walking towards the garage, Sinclair escorted his houseguest to the motorbike. On the way, Sanchez discovered in the hallway a framed Polaroid photograph of a young Sinclair, wearing a coat and standing next to an attractive dark young woman. She wore a coat, too, but it had apparently failed to insulate her from the cold ocean winds. He picked up the photo and looked at both of them. Alcatraz could be seen in the background, and Sanchez surmised that the photo was taken on the tour boat leaving the island.

"Sophie," Sinclair revealed her name.

Losing his grip, Sanchez almost dropped it.

"Don't worry," Sinclair kindly assured him. "It's fading, but I have it digitized. But I like the old-fashioned photo. It puts me in touch with my past. Fond memories, I guess."

"She's pretty," Sanchez commented as he put down the photo. "No . . . exotic."

"She's dead, too," Sinclair divulged sadly.

"Oh," Sanchez answered awkwardly. "Sorry."

"It's OK," Sinclair picked up the photo and looked at it. "She died in a car accident a few months after returning to Brazil. It happened long ago, but it seems like yesterday. What a cliché. But it's true."

Sanchez thought about what he could say to comfort Sinclair.

"Tough," he mumbled, feeling stupid.

"It is," Sinclair agreed and gently placed the photo down.

"You look really handsome," Sanchez tried to raise his spirits.

"And very young," Sinclair humorously added. "Well, . . . life gives us our time to be young."

Sanchez studied the photo and turned to Sinclair. "Your wife let you keep it here all these years?" he asked, curious.

"No," Sinclair laughed. "Otherwise I'd be divorced a long time ago. She was always jealous of Sophie's memory. Now, while she is gone, I can indulge in some nostalgia and sentimentality."

They remained silent for a long moment. "Let's go check out the bike," Sanchez suggested, reminding his mentor of their destination.

Sinclair happily led the way. Sanchez took one quick glance at the photograph before following Sinclair. They walked through the hallway and into the garage. Sinclair approached the motorbike and pointed to the engine.

"It's all done," he told Sanchez. "But it stalls out. Give it a try." Sanchez reluctantly accepted his invitation and straddled the bike.

"Look," Sinclair instructed him. "Take it out and pedal it like any other bike. Just keep the clutch open. It's the left handbrake." Sinclair squeezed the lever. "When you get it going real fast," he continued, "let go of the clutch. It will kick in and start."

Sanchez briefly took an assessment of the bike. He was uneasy; he had never ridden or driven an internal combustion machine. He carefully turned it around, depressing the clutch.

"Pedal fast," Sinclair reminded him.

He pushed the motorbike into the driveway and into the street. Seeing the street was empty, Sanchez followed Sinclair's instructions and began to pedal the bike fast. It accelerated up to ten miles an hour. "Let go of the clutch," Sinclair yelled from the driveway.

Sanchez let go of the clutch, and the motorbike started, ran for a few yards and sputtered. Sanchez repeated his effort several times, and the same engine failure occurred. Giving up, he pushed the motorbike back to the house.

"Can't get it going either?" Sinclair downheartedly asked, taking the motorbike's handlebars from Sanchez.

"No, but it's fixable," Sanchez concluded.

Sinclair looked at the motorbike and exhaled. "Maybe one day," Sinclair admitted. "I'll figure it out."

"It's really cool," Sanchez added. "When it gets going, how fast will it run?"

Sinclair did not immediately answer him as he pushed the motorbike into the garage. He parked it and covered the motorbike. Taking a long moment to look out into the street, Sinclair smiled and looked down at the motorbike without making eye contact with Sanchez. "As fast as it wants to go," he predicted. "As fast as it wants to go, my friend."

Chapter 21

May 2034
Sinclair

When Sinclair returned to school on Monday, the campus was in turmoil. Long lines of cars traveled in congested waves in front of the school. The spaces between the honking cars exposed marching lines of students holding signs. Recognizing many of the students streaming past him, Sinclair read the signs that protested against the recent cuts to the activity department's budget. Curious, he maneuvered his car close to a group of students being led by Asma. Perturbed, he read the club president's sign: "Save Stile's Memory. Resurrect our Clubs."

"Oh, shit," he said to himself.

Asma recognized Sinclair's car and began to jump up and down, screaming at the top of her lungs. "Mr. Sinclair," she shouted, waving her sign. "Woo!"

Sinclair waved to her and the other unruly students. Turning to the left, he carefully crossed the picket line of student protestors and passed a small circle of school police and media people. Several cameramen were walking among the students and interviewing them. Helicopters hovered low in the atmosphere. Once he entered the teachers' lot, he quickly parked and walked to the school entrance gate. The interior of the school campus stood empty. Although the students protested fifty yards away, their shouts and chatter reverberated across the lot to the entrance gate. When he entered the school, Pierce's secretary stood there, waiting to greet him.

"Pierce wants to see you for a moment," he told Sinclair. It was an order. He tried to object, but the secretary cut him off before he could open his mouth.

"The class is covered," he assured Sinclair. "Mr. Sanchez is there."

"I'm sure everyone showed up," Sinclair replied sarcastically.

The secretary gave Sinclair a disarming smile that signaled a mild threat. Sinclair had no options but to meet with Pierce.

"Of course," he answered and followed the secretary to Pierce's office.

There was an eerie, unnerving atmosphere in the administrators' office. Everyone was subdued. Sinclair followed the secretary to Pierce's door and knocked. Without waiting for an answer, he opened the door and escorted Sinclair to a chair where he remained standing. The secretary immediately stepped out, closing the door.

"Mr. Sinclair," Pierce stood up and gestured for him to sit. "Please."

He appeared flustered as the phone rang and he picked it up. "One second," Pierce pleaded. "Give me a few minutes, please. Yes. He's here. Thank you." He hung up and faced Sinclair.

"Mr. Sinclair" he began. "That was the superintendent's office. We're in a crisis mode." Sinclair nodded sympathetically but remained silent.

"Did you see those students outside?" he asked the obvious. His voice rose to a slight hysterical pitch.

"Yes," Sinclair answered, wishing to leave as soon as possible. "A small group."

Pierce gave him a look of consternation. "To make matters worse," he continued feverishly. "Stile's memorial service is tonight. The media circus is going to get worse, you know. I have a school to run and students to educate. This is not helping the situation."

"Yes," Sinclair repeated patiently, watching Pierce's hysteria mount.

Pierce glared at him and quickly looked down at his desk tablet. "I called you here because a source told me you inspired the protest," he spoke with alarm and gave Sinclair a weighty stare. "Is that correct?"

Stymied, Sinclair glared back at Pierce.

"Tell me!" Pierce demanded.

"I had no idea this was going to happen," he stated truthfully. "I only knew that the kids were upset. Asma has a very fiery personality. She gets excited about things at times."

"No, . . . she's a fanatic!" Pierce disputed. "More like an anarchist. She's behind this zoo." He pointed his finger in the general direction of the protestors on the street. "I just got out of a videoconference with the superintendent and his staff," he irately revealed the source of his frustration.

"In time, it will blow over," Sinclair said, trying to alleviate some of Pierce's dread.

Pierce did not immediately respond. "Not really," he disagreed. "We have an unfortunate death to contend with. They're saying the cuts killed him! Can you imagine?"

Sinclair watched him and felt sorry for the man. He was a pure technocrat who was never trained to handle any social or political crisis.

"How can I help?" Sinclair asked, hoping to deflate his anger.

Pierce looked up and expressed some relief at hearing his request. "I want you to talk to Asma," Pierce requested. "Have her come see me. We can sit around this afternoon and try to come to some arrangement."

Pierce's request surprised Sinclair. Pierce had missed the point of the protest. "This protest is not about you," Sinclair reminded him. "It's about the cuts. Unless you have a way to reinstate the money, she . . ."

"I still want to see her," Pierce demanded sharply, abruptly cutting off his advice. "I have authority to expel her, and the police can arrest her."

Sinclair forced himself to remain calm, and he took a long moment before giving his answer. "You should talk to your attorney," Sinclair advised. "She is a minor with constitutional rights. You might have another problem, . . . or the district might incur more legal headaches if you do something rash."

"Listen," Sinclair continued to speak. "She has her rights, but I am not responsible for her legal behavior. What can I say to her? She is protesting against the cuts. That's it! You're not responsible for his death."

"We are," Pierce retorted in a diplomatic tone. "In the arena of public opinion we are responsible. The media has made the decision on that end."

"I don't want anyone to be responsible for my death," Sinclair announced and stood up. "I'm sorry about your problem, but I have my own. Asma and the system need to work it out. I am not going to be the superintendent's bully." He stopped talking and he could feel his ears humming. They always hummed when his blood pressure peaked.

"Mr. Sinclair," Pierce addressed him sternly, "you are her sponsor. By the way, have you resolved your problem?"

"What?" Sinclair answered, confused. His mind had raced through his list of problems and challenges, and he could not make any immediate connection to Pierce's allusion.

"If you cooperate, . . . if you help us with this precocious child," Pierce carefully negotiated, "I am sure the superintendent . . . the district can help you with your . . . transition."

"Transition?" Sinclair repeated, grasping the meaning of Pierce's words.

Pierce provided a subtle nod.

"Thanks," he said acerbically. "I laid down my path already."

"Tread carefully," Pierce warned. "I am offering you some friendly advice. . . . Eighty years is a long time to be stuck in an unwanted place . . . or position. The offer comes from a reliable source."

"Bye," Sinclair dismissed himself and began to leave. "I'm gone."

"Mr. Sinclair," Pierce called after him.

Sinclair felt his anger rise as he left the room. Reviewing what had transpired in Pierce's office, he realized that someone somewhere was sending him a not-so-subtle message. He wondered how much input Mr. G had in recent events. In his mind, he knew he had made the right decision, even though the system and others would disagree. It was his own life, and he wanted something that gave his life its seminal definition. No one knew his final decision, and he wanted to announce it on his own terms. However, Sinclair felt that the time to do so was rapidly approaching, and he would have to change his plans slightly.

Outside, the protestors escalated their chants, and more helicopters appeared above the campus. Looking at the protestors,

Sinclair could see Asma rallying the students while carrying on a loud impromptu debate with the school police. Nearby, two camera operators trained their cameras on her. Even if Sinclair agreed with Pierce, he knew that any interference—when it came to Asma— would be futile. She would not listen and eventually she would convince him that she was right. The thought caused a mischievous smile to appear on his face. Sinclair suddenly felt a little better.

"Good job, girl," he congratulated her as he turned away and walked towards the lab where Sanchez was babysitting a small group of compliant students. "Maybe the time had finally come," he thought.

May Intermission

When Smith arrived at work, he opened his closet, and it was gone. He could not believe it. Dizzy, he felt his heart pounding furiously, and he went into a panic.

The samovar was missing from his closet.

Desperation drove him with a mindless fury to the refuse collection bins behind the school's gymnasium. On the way to the bins, he remembered that the refuse collectors would arrive later that day, a fact that gave him a slight hope. No thought of suspicion or castigation entered his mind. He only wanted to recover his samovar. When he got to the bins, he saw Kiki bent over and tugging at some unseen object.

"Is it there?" Smith screamed like a wailing child who had lost his mother.

Kiki instantly fell back and stared at Smith, who rushed forward.

"No me digas," he shouted, propelling himself toward the bin. "Don't tell me!"

Kiki stepped back as he dived into the bin.

"Smith," she advised him, "let me help."

Without waiting, she leaned over, grabbed one of the samovar's handles, and helped Smith yank it out of the bin. They hauled it over the ledge of the bin and set it down. Immediately, Smith removed a handkerchief and feverishly began to rub down and polish the samovar, while checking for any damage.

"I'm sorry," she tried to comfort him. "It looks OK."

Smith stopped polishing the samovar and looked up at her.

"This is not OK," Smith rejected her assessment of the situation. "No human being would do this to another person."

"He said it violated district policy," Kiki said, trying to mitigate the situation. "He was told to do it by the district engineer."

"No. Did the engineer tell Rubio to throw it into the refuse bin?" he challenged her excuse.

Kiki remained silent and fearful.

"This will not be forgiven," Smith promised her. "First, he offended my pride. The woman was the second wound, but now he stabs my heart. . . . Mi alma . . . My soul!"

"Cinderella?" Kiki questioned.

Smith ignored her. He stood up, pointed his index finger at his heart, and made a stabbing motion at his solar plexus.

He picked up his samovar and walked back to his closet. Kiki felt that she had to say something . . . to do something. Nevertheless, she was motionless; she knew that anything she said would be thrown back at her. She watched the old, defeated man embrace his samovar until he disappeared around the corner.

From a distance, she heard him begin to whistle the aria from his favorite opera.

At the house, Sanchez studied the motorbike. He had made several efforts to start the bike, but it consistently failed to turn over. Then he remembered his father who had owned an old Vespa. After making a short search through the garage, he found a flat head screwdriver and returned to the motorbike. Looking for the carburetor, he found the adjustment screw that regulated the fuel and air mixture. He turned the screw to the right and tried to start the motorbike. Straddling the bike, he began to pedal and hoped it would run smoothly. Usually, the motorbike would start and die. Now it did nothing. Exhausted, Sanchez stopped pedaling. He returned to the garage and used the screwdriver to turn the adjustment screw to the left beyond its original point. Pedaling the motorbike again, he was able to start it immediately and maintain a running bike. The machine steadily accelerated up to 25 mph.

"Woo!" he roared, holding up an arm. "Woo!"

I Have Three Things to Tell You, My Friend

The motorbike chugged like an old Weedwacker, but it sounded like an harmonious concerto to Sanchez. Some neighbors exited their homes to see what Sanchez was doing, and a few waved and smiled. Most people had not seen a gas engine in years. He made a U-turn and parked the motorbike in the garage. Placing it back on its stand, he let it idle for a while.

"Wow!" he bellowed victoriously. "So easy. Wow!"

He released the clutch lever, and the motorbike stopped gruffly. The smell of engine oil and gas exhaust wafted through the garage. Sanchez inhaled the smell and enjoyed the aftereffect of his success. He could not wait to tell Sinclair, but he wanted to do it in person— when Sinclair came home. Seeing his greasy and dirty hands, he decided to clean the bike and then shower. There were no towels in the garage, so he entered the house and looked for cleaning solutions and cloths. Inside, Sanchez again spied the old Polaroid photo. He picked it up and stared at it. He enjoyed looking at Sinclair's happy and youthful expression. He also wondered about Sophie. Who was she? He had so many questions for Sinclair . . . when the time came.

Then he felt it. Behind the picture frame, under the felt, there was a slight protuberance. Peeling off the felt back, he extracted an old-style postcard. Holding up the card, Sanchez read a note Sophie had sent to Sinclair from Brazil. He reread it several times and then carefully returned it to the frame. The postcard had answered some of his questions. If the opportunity presented itself, Sanchez would ask Sinclair about Sophie that evening.

But for some unknown reason, Sinclair never arrived home that weekend.

Chapter 22

June 2034
Smith

"Now I'm ready to tell you."
—Fernando Smith (The Janitor)

Everyone saw him. He first appeared among the protestors. Later the media crew and the police saw him. When he showed off his costume, they all welcomed him and laughed. Everyone thought it was a great stunt until the first shot rang. Soon, more shots were fired . . . then, silence.

By the time Sinclair arrived late to school, the protestors had vanished, but the sky swarmed with buzzing, agitated helicopters and bands of sycophant media crews begging for information and access to the school. A squadron of police kept the media and others away, including the teachers and students who were milling about in the parking lot. Sinclair parked his car, and before he could reach the entrance, a small crowd of students accosted him. They were anxious to tell him about the shocking events inside the school.

"Did you hear?" they all shouted in unison.

"No!" he snapped back.

"He killed them!" they spoke spontaneously. "Just killed them. . . . That's what we heard."

"Who?" Sinclair demanded to know. "Who killed who?"

"That crazy guy," one student yelled back.

"He creeped me out," another female student said.

"Bang," a football player coughed aloud. He smiled maliciously in Sinclair's direction.

"It was Smith. The janitor," Laura gently told him when he reached the security line. "They won't let us in."

Several media people managed to reach the front line of students and staff. They were posing questions to anyone who would speak to them.

"I can see," Sinclair said, noticing the tumult of students, teachers, and journalists. He wondered why Smith would have shot anyone. "What happened?"

"I don't know," Laura admitted and shrugged. "It's the system, you know."

Sinclair stared at her and tried to search for the meaning of her statement, but the school police officer interrupted his thoughts.

"Sinclair!" he called out.

Sinclair looked up to see who had called him, and the police officer waved him to come in. A small break in the security line allowed him just enough space to walk through the crowd.

"Hurry," the officer urged him. "Pierce wants to talk to you."

"Sinclair," a familiar voice in the crowd shouted. "Where have you been?"

Sinclair briefly turned around to find Sanchez waving his arms.

"Take care of my motorbike," he ordered Sanchez and waved back.

"It runs," Sanchez broadcast the information proudly. "It runs."

Sinclair gave him a thumbs-up and waved again.

"I knew you would do it," he complimented Sanchez.

Privately, Sinclair could not fathom the secret of Sanchez's mechanical miracle. It irked him not to know how he had fixed it.

Instantly, a team of media cameramen and reporters dashed forward and knocked aside several teachers and students.

"Hey," they shouted in Sinclair's direction. "Tell us what's going on?"

Sinclair caught one cameraman pointing his camera in his direction. He held it on Sinclair until the security line reformed, eclipsing Sinclair from the view of the curious crowd. Above, the media helicopters converged on the entrance. As Sinclair walked towards the entrance, he could still hear the questions being shouted in his direction.

"Go, Sinclair," a student shouted over the roar of the media people.

Unlike the noise outside, a disquieting stillness permeated the classrooms and hallways, and dread could be felt in the steely presence of security officers and assault teams. The muffled sting of mutilated voices crackled intermittently, escaping from various communication devices clipped to thick utility belts. The police officer escorted Sinclair into the administration building and through another layer of tactical police officers and their support team. Inside, the offices hummed with more activity. As he approached Pierce's office, no one gave him a second look as the officers concentrated on their tablets or communication devices. In the far corner, Sinclair noticed several officers, dressed in military uniforms, load ammunition and gas canisters into magazine wells.

"He's waiting with the chief," the police officer opened Pierce's door.

Sinclair was exhausted. He did not bother to ask who the chief was, but he suspected that it was the district's chief of police or the urban chief. When he entered, he saw that he was correct. All were there: Pierce, the urban chief, the district chief, Counselor Vega, and a military colonel were all gathered around Pierce's desk. Their presence diminished the size of the room, making it seem compact and stifling. In the corner, Sinclair saw a subdued Asma, sitting nervously next to Vega who had been comforting her.

"Sit down," Pierce ordered. "You look a bit disheveled."

"I'll be OK," Sinclair assured him. "Long weekend . . . taking care of some stuff."

Asma cheered up at seeing Sinclair, and Vega displayed a smile of relief. Sinclair squeezed into the only empty chair in front of Pierce who was flanked by the police officers and the military representative.

"Let's come to the point," the colonel announced without ceremony. "We have a crisis. . . . Maybe a hostage situation."

"I can see," Sinclair responded sourly, looking around the room and forcing a smile for Asma.

"This is Col. Esparra," Pierce introduced the colonel. "And District Chief Barbara Pagan and Urban Chief Nick Rice."

The police chiefs nodded politely.

"Please, Mr. Pierce," Esparra interrupted. "We have a situation."

Sinclair examined the police chiefs who appeared calmly solemn in contrast to Esparra's agitated demeanor.

"We don't know about hostages," Urban Chief Nick Rice corrected her. "Maybe not."

"Mr. Sinclair," Pierce interrupted, attempting to diffuse the tension between Esparra and Rice. "He wants to see you."

"He?" Sinclair asked.

"You know," Pierce spoke angrily. "That crazy janitor, . . . Smith."

"He is a venomous little creature," Esparra disparaged Smith. "I read his bio."

Pierce gave her a disapproving look.

"We're wasting time," Esparra reminded Pierce. "My soldiers are ready."

Sinclair recalled observing the soldiers load their weapons outside the office.

"Wait," Pierce warned, raising his hand as a signal for her to desist. "This is still in our jurisdiction."

Pierce looked at District Chief Pagan, who nodded in agreement.

"We have full authority," she reminded the colonel.

"OK," Esparra accepted the situation. "But not for long. . . . The longer you wait, the more likely the governor will turn the situation over to me."

Pierce gave her a menacing look and then addressed Sinclair.

"He wants to see you," Pierce explained again. "Smith."

Asma's face became animated, and she tried to make eye contact with Pierce.

"How do you know?" Sinclair continued to ask.

"He told her," Pierce pointed to Asma. "And he called here a couple of times."

"You talked to him?" Sinclair was surprised.

"Let the girl tell him," Pagan suggested.

"We're wasting time," Esparra repeated.

Everyone ignored her and turned instead to Asma. Vega touched her hand, and she looked directly at Sinclair who returned a sympathetic smile.

"Tell him what happened," Pierce encouraged her.

Her eyes began to water, but she managed to hold back her tears. Sinclair had never seen her so emotionally distraught—so contrary to her normal behavior.

"Mr. Sinclair," she pleaded. "I couldn't do anything."

"It's OK," he comforted her. "Take your time."

She looked at Vega and then sat upright in her chair.

"I saw the janitor wearing this clown suit," she recalled. "It was the kind that looked like a harlequin with a ball of yarn on top of his cap. The rest of the clown costume was a white jumpsuit with red and blue polka dots."

Esparra sighed impatiently, but Asma ignored her.

"He opened his room and sat inside. Sometimes he cursed," she continued shakily. "And then Mr. Rubio showed up. He yelled at the janitor, and then I heard a brief argument. I couldn't make it out. It was in Spanish."

She stopped to catch her breath.

"He then shot him," Asma added sadly. "Right at the door when Mr. Rubio was leaving. I watched him drag the body in. So, . . . I don't know why, . . . but I followed him into the closet. That's when I saw her."

She dropped her head. Sinclair could hear her whimper.

"Please," Pierce encouraged her to continue.

Burying her face in her hands, she continued with her description of the scene.

"I don't know," Asma cried. "I felt like I was being pulled in."

She looked up at Sinclair with terrified eyes.

"When I got closer," she continued, "then I saw her."

"Who?" Sinclair began to lose his patience.

"That female janitor. The pretty one," Asma said irritably. "She had a knife in her chest. There was blood all over. It looked like he stabbed her a lot. It was horrible."

She began to cry.

"She was an employee," Pierce named the victim. "Helen Rivas, one of our janitors."

"Why is she here?" Sinclair questioned the wisdom of keeping Asma present in Pierce's office. She cried a little longer but then stopped. Pagan and Rice appeared suddenly agitated, and Esparra's eyes bulged with resentment and anger.

"She insisted on telling you," Pierce answered.

"He saw me," she explained in a low voice. "Then he said, 'Go get Sinclair, little girl.' He held up this bloody knife. I saw the gun next to the samovar."

"Me?" Sinclair rejected the request. "Why does he want to see me?"

"Mr. Vega," Pierce halted the conversation. "Please take Asma to your office. Her parents are waiting."

"I'm sorry, Mr. Sinclair," Asma pleaded and began to walk to the door with the support of Vega.

Sinclair stood up and gently hugged her as she left the office. When they were gone, Pierce stood and checked the lock on the door. Leaning on the edge of his desk, he faced Sinclair.

"I can't send you," Pierce explained the situation. "But he wants to see you."

"Bad idea," Esparra objected. "My team can take him out."

"Not with a bomb," Pagan reminded everyone. "He told the girl he has a bomb in that teapot!"

"Really?" Sinclair was doubtful. "How do you know it's a bomb? Have you thought that he's crazy?"

"We don't know," Pierce concurred. "But if he does, . . . it can get worse."

"It's already out of control," Esparra reminded everyone. "He has a gun, doesn't he? How did he get a gun? They've been banned."

The police chiefs both looked askance at her blatant naïveté.

"Do you know anything about this other janitor and Rubio?" Pierce inquired directly, losing patience with Esparra.

Sinclair thought for a second and made an assumption.

"I guess the girl and Rubio had something going on," Sinclair assumed. "He found out and felt . . . real bad. I know he was in love with her. He spoke to my TA about her, too. Sanchez."

"Shit!" Rice cursed. "He's also a lovesick crazy."

"But why me?" Sinclair asked desperately, trying to comprehend his summons.

"We think maybe you can talk him out of it, . . ." Pierce admitted, "to surrender."

He looked at Pagan who remained stoically unmoved.

"He will kill this man, too," Esparra disagreed vehemently, slapping her hands with a loud clap. "He wants another hostage. Or just a hostage."

"Maybe," Sinclair almost agreed. "But I know he really wants to talk. Something is on his mind, and he wants to tell me. I'm guessing from past conversations. But I'm not a shrink. This is very unpredictable."

"Do you know anything about the clown outfit?" Rice asked.

"Pervert!" Esparra exclaimed.

Sinclair gave her a look of disgust before answering.

"No," he told them. "But I know enough that it has a purpose. The man is highly self-educated."

"He has no professional degrees," Pierce pointed out.

Sinclair smiled and chuckled to himself. "He reads voraciously," Sinclair said. "He is also an avid fan of classical music, especially opera. That man has a mind like a search engine. You can ask him anything, and he will know something about it."

"Crazy and smart," Pagan negatively concluded. "Shit! Who hired this bastard?"

They ignored the rhetorical question.

Pierce leaned over and put his hand on Sinclair's shoulder. "I want to know if you'll..." he began to ask. "You don't have to. . . . We understand."

He studied the facial expressions of the two police chiefs, and they nodded agreeably.

"No!" Esparra rejected the suggestion. "It's irregular."

"Technically," Pierce corrected her, "Mr. Sinclair is his legal representative . . . the union rep."

"No," Esparra vetoed the allusion, "you can't pawn that off in this situation. There are no legal grounds. Mr. Sinclair is an employee and a civilian. You are taking some grave legal responsibilities in this matter."

"I told you," Pagan rebuked her, "we are the authority, . . . and the governor hasn't made a decision. Mr. Sinclair can be . . . technically deputized."

Sinclair shot Pierce a skeptical glare.

"I'm calling the governor," Esparra announced furiously. "This amateur hour has to end!" She gave Pierce a threatening look and ran out of the office in a huff. They silently watched her leave.

"She's on the phone with the governor now," Pagan commented. "I can't ask you to go, Mr. Sinclair, . . . but I wouldn't go. I gave her that line to keep them out of our cookie jar. I don't like her." Sinclair studied her expression, but she showed no emotion, only firm resolve.

"Mr. Sinclair," Pierce said, breaking the silence. "I am not sure about a hostage, . . . but I know you can help. You have a rapport with Smith. I remember the union conferences. He respects you."

"You're asking me to go?" Sinclair challenged him. Pierce shifted his eyes away from Sinclair and glanced at the two police chiefs. "I'm going anyway," he decided. Pierce expressed his approval.

"I think we can resolve this," Pierce said, seeking approval from the two police chiefs who declined to give their assent. Sinclair read their vacuous expressions and ignored them. They wanted to leave no official fingerprints on the matter.

"Don't I need to be deputized?" Sinclair asked flippantly. He made eye contact with the Pagan, who grinned slyly.

"It's meaningless," Pagan admitted and stood up. She extended her hand to Sinclair, and he shook it. "Do it quickly if you are determined. The tactical team will go in within the hour. Maybe less time, I think, if Esparra has her way."

Sinclair felt that her prediction was accurate. "How do I get there?" he asked, knowing the level of tight security. "Not alone?"

"I'll have an officer escort you to the lab," Pagan assured him. "You'll have clearance."

She remembered something else. "Do you want some nonlethal weapon?" she asked. "A Taser?"

"No," Sinclair declined and stood up. "It would provoke him if he finds out."

She nodded in agreement.

"Sinclair," Pierce said, suddenly having some doubts. "You don't have to, . . . you know."

"I have to," Sinclair assured him. "It's my decision. Do you think he has a bomb?" He looked at them all, and they remained impassive. No one answered; no one knew.

"He found a weapon," Rice said, bluntly validating Smith's resourcefulness. "Anything is possible."

"I feel you can help," Pierce said feebly and tried to offer Sinclair some consolation for his decision. "Maybe you can diffuse the situation . . . no pun intended."

Sinclair chuckled, stood up, waved, and turned around. Pagan followed him out of the room, but he felt further discussions were useless.

"I'm calling Smith to tell him you're coming," Pierce promised as Sinclair departed. "We don't want to surprise him."

Sinclair did not turn around to respond as he stepped out with Pagan. "Take Mr. Sinclair to the lab," she told an officer who had immediately approached and saluted. "I'll clear the way."

A short distance away, Sinclair and Pagan witnessed Esparra, having a passionate conversation on her cellphone with a representative from the governor's office. Everyone eavesdropped but pretended not to listen.

"Any time now," the Pagan warned Sinclair. She gently touched Sinclair's hand. "Good luck," she offered.

"Yeah," Sinclair accepted and hesitantly accompanied the police officer to the school's quad.

District and urban police, scattered around the building, had barricaded the school. Sinclair thought about how quickly a place could change from an institution of learning, with happy, energized adolescents, to an environment of fear and terror. Some police seemed anxious, while others displayed belligerence. Sinclair could smell blood. They wanted to kill because murder was rare in their time. An opportunity to murder would never come again.

"Let's go," the officer called to Sinclair who had stalled in front of the lab's hallway. "Good luck. You are going in alone from here."

They shook hands, and the officer opened the door to allow Sinclair to pass alone through the doorway. Once inside, he was in darkness as the shaft of outdoor sunlight collapsed when the police officer closed the door. Sinclair stood quietly at the end of the hallway. He was alone. Another shaft of light pierced the darkness from the opposite direction.

"Come in," Smith's voice called from the end of the other hallway. "Hurry, my friend."

Sinclair felt ill, but he pushed down the bile in his throat as he struggled to stroll carefully down the chiaroscuro hallway. The atmosphere seemed like an old movie western scene, when the gunslinger faced his opponent at the end of the road. A long time seemed to pass before Sinclair reached the closet. Smith's silhouette was blocking some of the interior light as he stood holding an antique brass dragoon pistol and wearing the clown suit in homage to his favorite opera. Asma was correct in her description.

"Old," Smith said, referring to the black powder revolver he held up. "But it works. A replica of an old Colt Walker. I picked it up from an antique shop long ago. You don't need a license. By law, it's antiquated, like a bow and arrow."

Smith waved Sinclair inside and waited for him to enter before he closed the closet's door. Inside, Sinclair smelled cleaning chemicals, a faint trace of gunpowder, and tea. A mild stench of blood also greeted him.

"Watch out," Smith said, pointing to bloodstains to the right of the samovar. "I cleared the area. Sit here. It's clean."

Sinclair looked around and saw that Smith had rearranged the room. The two bodies were nowhere to be seen.

"The bodies?" Smith understood his thoughts. "I moved them to the lab. They don't deserve to be where honorable people sit."

Smith pointed his dragoon at the empty seat. "Sit," he softly ordered, "my friend."

Reluctantly, Sinclair sat next to the samovar, and Smith holstered his gun in his belt. Taking a clean porcelain cup out of a drawer, he served Sinclair some tea.

"Last time, I'm afraid," he spoke sadly and sat down next to Sinclair. "I'm sorry the girl saw all the death, but . . . that is life. What a pity."

Holding the cup of tea, Sinclair stared in confusion at Smith who tranquilly drank his tea. "The tactical team will come in soon," Sinclair warned him. "There's this colonel who's talking to the governor."

"I'll let you go when we hear them come storming in," Smith assured Sinclair. He pulled out his dragoon with his free hand and held it up. "I still have some shots left. The .44 caliber slugs are still bad for the health." Smith snickered at his private joke and holstered his gun again.

"So why?" Sinclair asked the obvious.

"Drink," Smith commanded sternly.

Intimidated, Sinclair forced himself to lift the cup to his lips and take a sip. Smith joined him.

"Good," Smith said, satisfactorily.

Sinclair felt like vomiting.

"I will tell you why," Smith revealed. "So you tell all those motherfuckers out there the truth. They are already lying about me."

He then drank as he brooded, and he noticed that Sinclair was staring at his costume.

"Oh this?" Smith noticed and sniggered, proudly touching his costume. "I'm the victim . . . the clown. But I am not a fool! I told her and that . . . fornicator."

Smith grabbed the top of his cap and took it off, waving it for a moment and then placing it back on his head.

"I am not a fool," he repeated. "Life is a comedy or tragedy. You know, a comedy is a tragedy with a happy conclusion. I want my tragedy to have a happy ending . . . on my terms." He produced a small bottle of hard liquor and poured some of it into his cup of tea.

"She," he motioned the cup in the direction of the lab, "betrayed me. I felt it, but I wouldn't believe it. Then I saw the kid's video. I got the video. Paid for it! And I saw her . . . with that man. She's no Cinderella."

"Rubio?" Sinclair questioned.

Smith glared at him, and his cup trembled.

"That fucker," Smith continued, looking beyond Sinclair at some distant point. "He abused me . . . ridiculed me . . . and then betrayed her . . . and me. Then he did worse. . . . He threw away my samovar. That wounded me. He died too easy. Too easy! He almost stopped my legal rehabilitation. The bastard!"

"She didn't?" Sinclair awkwardly inquired.

"No," Smith spoke factually. "The whore didn't die easy. It was slow. All blood here. She broke my heart."

"You're a murderer," Sinclair accused him. "She didn't deserve death. People have a right to do what they want."

"As long as they don't hurt others," Smith disagreed sternly. He returned to his drink and swallowed its contents. Producing the bottle of hard liquor again, he took a swig. "She would die a thousand more times," Smith added grudgingly and drank again. "If I could bring her back to life. Bitch."

Sinclair wondered how Smith had acquired the video from a student and what the video showed. A small shout from outside stopped him from asking Smith any more details.

"Bomb?" Sinclair spat out the first word that came to his mind. "They say you have a bomb?"

"You are well informed," Smith congratulated him and saluted him with his drink. "Yes. A big one! It's a chemical bomb. . . . Don't worry; it'll evaporate me and everything around here. Boom! They are so stupid. You can't ban anything from people who think."

Smith reached over and turned on his music. His old Leoncavallo arias played with a disheartened languor.

"So you want me to tell them you're a victim?' Sinclair clarified. He felt slightly dizzy.

"Yes," Smith concurred. "You know how to talk. You're a good talker." Smith inquisitively studied Sinclair and weighed his next words. Outside, the sounds of shouting officers increased. "I have a question for you?" Smith asked forlornly.

Sinclair briefly lost his focus but recovered. "What?" Sinclair almost slurred.

"You have made a decision?" Smith asked, smiling as he took a drink. "Were you going to go to rehabilitation?"

Sinclair hesitated and then answered. "No," he said. "I decided to grow old and die on my own time."

"Then," Smith continued asking his questions, "when do you want to die?"

"What?" Smith asked, confused.

"It's the tea," Smith revealed amusingly. "You can let the tea kill you slowly or you can die here."

"What?' Sinclair raised his voice and tried to stand up. He fell down into his seat. "You poisoned me?"

"They had already poisoned you," Smith argued, "with their rehabilitation shit! Don't worry. There's not enough to kill you before you tell my story. You should thank me."

Sinclair looked at his cup and slammed it against the samovar where it shattered.

Smith shrugged indifferently. "You see," he observed, "sometimes we have to react."

"You bastard," Sinclair cursed. Despite the halo of the drug, Sinclair could hear movement at the end in the hallway. Esparra had gotten her way with the governor, and District Chief Pagan was right. Sinclair knew they would not be alone for very long.

"So decide," Smith again challenged him. "Go the easy way or go as a public victim of a crazy *Pagliaccio*."

Smith's words danced and stalled in Sinclair's head, and he tried to connect them into sentences and meaning. His mind kept drifting to the hallway where more noise could be heard.

"Make it quick," Smith urged him. "You have to leave now, . . . or I'll end up killing more people."

Sinclair saw Smith produce a small electrical switch that had once served as a light switch.

"I had to improvise," Smith said proudly. "You know how this will end. You made your decision to die. Why prolong it? Why drag it out? Look, I did you a favor, my friend. You can die knowing I killed you. But you can have one more decision. That I give to you. Time is ending soon. Decide quickly. ¡Ahora!"

The noise escalated in the hallway, as Esparra's team prepared to make a move. But they too had to decide.

"Smith," a robotic voice warned the janitor from the end of the hallway. "Let Mr. Sinclair go. We can talk."

Suddenly the phone rang. Smith ignored it. It stopped. Then it rang again. Sinclair looked at the phone and at Smith. "Decide," Smith insisted, holding up the switch.

Sinclair felt some difficulty breathing, but he was not in pain. . . . He was dying. Glumly, he realized that death was inevitable. It might be the better way. The future was closed. He grunted and dipped his head.

Smith understood.

"Good choice," he accepted his decision graciously and held the switch up. "They can believe what they want. This comedy is over, my friend."

From outside, the tactical team saw a blinding flash of light an instant before a wave of searing heat washed down the hallway. Instantaneously, a thunderous explosion erupted and vaporized a third of the virtual lab. Later, investigators thought that a miracle had saved the tactical team; only a few officers had received minor injuries. Among the remains, the forensic team was able to recover only shards of the samovar and pieces of the old Colt Walker dragoon.

Postscript

June 2084
Sanchez

Sanchez, facing rehabilitation, found the old Polaroid in his stored collections as he packed. He had forgotten about the photo but not the postcard. Alone, he studied the milky photograph for a long while and then turned it over, gently removing the postcard from the frame. After forty years, he revisited Sophie's final greeting.

I'm coming home to you, my love. Boa noite e bons sonhos.

Sanchez read it over several times before turning over the postcard and studying the photo of Rio's Christ the Redeemer.

"Miss you, my friend," Sanchez, feeling mawkish, told his old mentor.

Carefully, he returned the postcard to where it had always belonged . . . in the past.

"Good night and sweet dreams."

About the Author

RM DAmato received a B.A. from California State University, Northridge in 1982 and an M.A. from U.S.C. in 1983. He worked as an assistant editor for the Los Angeles Times and executive recruiter for Fortune 100 companies. Currently, he is an adjunct professor at Miami Dade College. His previous novel, *The Last Seminarian*, was a finalist for Foreword Magazine's 'Science Fiction Book of the Year' award. He is also the author of a collection of poetry, *The Musings of a Late Baby Boomer*.

Also by RM DAmato

**Finalist for Foreword Magazine's 2013 Book of the Year Award.
#1 Amazon bestseller.**

The year is 2040. Facing the threat of a viral pandemic, four friends will finally unite for an extraordinary reunion. Within an orbiting virtual world, the former seminarians will confront personal demons, while sharing ideas about the meaning of life, friendship, and love—including the existence of god. It is an allegorical dance played out in the microcosmic and metaphysical drama of the human condition. Can they return to Earth before the plague makes it impossible, dropping the curtain on existence forever?

Random Musings of a Late Baby Boomer explores personal and seminal moments from the early 1960s until the present. Adapting free verse style and conversational tones, the poems meditate upon the universal and existential questions that produce the events that "rub" a life. *Random Musings* rouses the dormant mind and slinks alongside the periphery of space's cold, black abyss with a hot dog as a companion.